To my reader — Claiming you! ♡ Happy reading!

Naima Simone

BEAUTY AND THE BACHELOR

A BACHELOR AUCTION NOVEL

NAIMA SIMONE

Entangled Publishing, LLC
2614 South Timberline Road
Suite 109
Fort Collins, CO 80525
Visit our website at www.entangledpublishing.com.

Indulgence is an imprint of Entangled Publishing, LLC.

Edited by Tracy Montoya
Cover design by Kelley York
Cover art from Shutterstock

Manufactured in the United States of America

First Edition August 2015

To Gary. 143.

Chapter One

During Lucas Oliver's first week as a new transfer student to the Chicago public school system, he'd witnessed a fight between a kid who should've been a sophomore in college, not high school, and a tall, skinny freshman.

Well…"fight" was a bit of a misnomer.

The skinny kid, Terrance Wallace, had tried to walk away—probably applying that "turn the other cheek" rhetoric he'd learned in Sunday school. He'd ended up sprawled on the floor, that cheek busted.

The following year, Terrance returned to school beefed up and full of 'roid rage. The prey had suddenly become the predator, handing out the same beatdowns he used to suffer.

Lucas had learned two valuable lessons then. Well, two and a half.

One. Get before you get got.

Two. Preparation is the key to successful revenge.

Two and a half. Steroids are some nasty shit.

Now, years later, standing in a crowded ballroom at an event hosted by the Rhodonite Society, a philanthropic organization comprised of Boston's wealthy elite, Lucas possessed an affinity for Terrance. True, Lucas's own revenge plan had taken considerably more time to set in motion than a summer of pumping weights and shooting up. Fifteen years longer.

Still, as he hovered on the cusp of realizing his dream of retribution, reflecting on every long, hard year felt sweet. As sweet as it must've been for Terrance to plant his fist in the mouth of the thug who'd made his life a living hell.

He lightly traced the thin, flattened ridge of scar tissue under his right eye, picturing its twin that bisected his eyebrow. Bitterness throbbed inside him like a wound unable to heal because his memories insisted on ripping off the scab, keeping the injury fresh and angry.

Every scar. Every agony. Every humiliation. Every moment of fear—they were all worth this moment. He watched his quarry hold court among his peers, laughing and basking in his power, his glory, completely unaware he was being hunted. This moment of happiness would be the man's last before he suffered the same pain and devastation he'd so carelessly meted out to others.

Lucas studied the face of the man who'd betrayed Lucas's family so deeply, the scars on his face didn't compare to the ones carved into his soul.

And smiled.

"Oh, shit, you're smiling," a voice said to his left.

He slid a sidelong glance at Aiden Kent, his business partner and best friend since high school. Hell, his only friend. Most people called Lucas the Beast of Bay Bridge

Industries—or "cold-blooded," "bastard," or "son of a bitch." But not "friend."

"Since you've ignored my advice up until this point, I'm not holding out hope you'll listen to me at this late date. But, once again, I'm going to put it out there. I don't agree with this," Aiden stated. "Buy his business, ruin his reputation. Those are fair game. But you should leave his daughter out of it. She's innocent."

Lucas glanced across the room again, his gaze landing on the "she" Aiden mentioned. Statuesque. Elegant. Hair straight as a ruler and the color of sun-bleached wood. Skin like the richest, purest honey.

And guilty by association.

"Your concern is duly noted…again," Lucas drawled.

Aiden swore under his breath. "All this damn intrigue." He shook his head, his eyes troubled. "There's something about you blue bloods with your plots and schemes. Us blue-collar folk? We might not have been born with silver spoons in our mouths or McMansions on the Gold Coast, but at least you can immediately tell if we don't like you. A fist to the face transcends race, religion, creed, and social and economic lines."

"I'm not a blue blood," Lucas stated flatly, tone carefully void of emotion.

Aiden sighed. "You were born into the same world these people live in, even though the streets of Chicago raised you as they did me. Still, the tax bracket your parents belonged to doesn't make you any less, or more, of a man. But what you've set in motion here"—he nodded in the direction of the man and woman under discussion—"doesn't speak to the person you've become. Luke, let the rage and hatred go before it eats you alive and leaves you with nothing."

You have no idea what the hell you're talking about.

The words surged to the back of his throat, scalding the lining like bile. But he swallowed the hot rebuke. Aiden might have been born and raised in Chicago's rough South Side, but somehow his spirit hadn't been sullied with a bitterness that had been embedded inside Lucas since he lost his family at fourteen. And also underneath the unsolicited kumbaya-why-can't-we-all-just-get-along advice, he detected Aiden's affection and love. And worry.

"I made a promise, and I'm not going back on it. Not even for you or my highly debatable soul."

"Oh, you have a soul," his friend scoffed. "It might be a little charred around the edges, but it's there." Aiden scrubbed a hand over the back of his neck. "Fine. I can't talk you out of going through with it. But just…be careful. Ever hear the saying, 'Unforgiveness is like drinking a poison and hoping the other person dies'?"

Lucas stared at Aiden. Blinked. "What the hell? Did you read a box of Hallmark cards before coming here tonight?"

"You know the redhead I met last week?" Aiden shrugged a shoulder. "She was watching Dr. Phil earlier. The show was about warring in-laws, but I thought the quote seemed appropriate for the situation."

Lucas snorted. "I remember her. What worries me is you were with a gorgeous woman, and the only thing you could find interesting to do was watch Dr. Phil."

"Unlike you, I know there's more to romance than sex." He clapped Lucas on the shoulder. "I'm out. Only ten of these women will leave with a bachelor. The others will need consolation."

"Real romantic," Lucas called after him.

With a wicked grin, Aiden walked away, and damned if several appreciative gazes didn't follow him. The attention didn't surprise Lucas. With his dark blond hair, green eyes, and classically handsome features, Aiden drew women like flies to shit. Not that Lucas had ever experienced any problem attracting women, either. Aiden was just prettier to look at.

He slid his hands into the pockets of his tuxedo pants and returned his attention to the older man surrounded by family, friends, and those who wished they were friends.

Pleasure stole through him, filling him like the hearty beef-and-carrot stew his uncle used to cook on the coldest Chicago winter nights. Thick. Warm.

Satisfying.

Fifteen years.

It'd taken fifteen years, but finally Jason Blake would pay for everything he'd cost Lucas.

His childhood.

His legacy.

His father.

Chapter Two

"Welcome to the Rhodonite Society's tenth annual Masquerade Bachelor Auction." The cultured voice of the mistress of ceremonies echoed throughout the brightly lit ballroom. "We have a fabulous night planned for you. In just a few minutes, ten of the most handsome and *eligible* bachelors the city of Boston has to offer will take the stage offering ten romantic, luxurious dates! And every penny of the proceeds will benefit the Blake Literacy Foundation, which raises awareness of illiteracy as well as provide programming, tutoring, and technology to Boston's underprivileged youth. So bidders, have your checkbooks ready!"

As the MC's announcement gave way to excited chatter, Sydney Blake worked to maintain the gracious smile ingrained in her since she was old enough for tea parties with her dolls: a polite curve of the mouth with the corners tipped just enough to be demure but not so much to appear garish or bold.

A perfect lady's smile. For the perfect daughter. For the

perfect fiancée.

Lie. Lie. Lie.

"I am absolutely determined to go home with a bachelor this evening. Of course, some of us don't have to worry about snagging a handsome, rich man. I heard congratulations are in order, Sydney." A young blonde with the sharp, dangerous beauty of a bejeweled sword purred and air-kissed Sydney's cheeks. "I was so delighted to hear about your engagement."

"You two make such a beautiful couple," a stunning brunette cooed. "Your wedding is bound to be the biggest social event of the year. Have you set a date yet?"

Sydney murmured a "thank you" and a "not yet" as the other woman clasped Sydney's hand and elevated it so light from the chandelier bounced off the three-carat diamond solitaire. *Wow. Really?* Squelching the spurt of irritation, she pressed her tongue to the roof of her mouth, saying nothing. Still…if the other woman snatched out a jeweler's loupe, all bets were off.

"How beautiful," the blonde murmured, her expression warm, but the ice in her eyes matched the hardness of the gem weighing down Sydney's finger. "You're so fortunate." While stated in a sugary, butter-won't-melt-in-your-mouth voice, the barb possessed razor-sharp teeth.

"Yes, we are fortunate to add Tyler to our family," Sydney's father, Jason Blake, boasted with a broad grin. Hurt, embarrassment, and a weary resentment swarmed over her skin and swirled in her chest like an aggravated hive of bees. *They* were lucky. Not, "Yes, Tyler is indeed fortunate to have my daughter for his wife," as other proud fathers would've bragged. God, after so many years, she should be accustomed to his casual dismissal of her. Yet even at twenty-five years old, she hadn't managed to develop that Teflon skin required to deflect the offhand barbs and comments that were part and parcel of possessing a vagina in the Blake household.

But, really, what did she have to complain about? Her fiancé ~~was~~ ~~the~~ only son of real estate mogul Wes Reinhold, and heir to the Reinhold financial empire. Her father was *ecstatic* Sydney had finally done something to prove herself worthy of the Blake name.

"Where is the happy groom-to-be?" the blonde asked, her greedy gaze scanning the crowded ballroom.

"He's graciously volunteered to participate in the auction tonight. Already supporting the family," Charlene Blake, Sydney's mother, explained. Every year, proceeds from the Rhodonite Society's annual Masquerade Bachelor Auction benefited the Blake family's literacy foundation. Tyler's inclusion in the popular auction was just another tick in the Tyler's-the-perfect-son-in-law column.

"Oh, how sweet," the blonde purred.

Yes. Sweet. Of course, the mistress of ceremonies had already pulled Sydney aside and provided her with Tyler's number to ensure Sydney would win his company for the evening.

According to her mother, there was altruism and then there was stupidity. And apparently, trusting her fiancé with a woman like the hungry, flinty-eyed blonde for the length of an evening weighed on the unforgivable side of foolishness.

"If you'll excuse us, we need to go to our table," Sydney said, glancing toward the stage and the subtle flickering of the lights. Thank God. Her nice-nasty limit was fast approaching critical mass.

Murmuring a final good night, she headed to the table reserved for her family. Skirting a cluster of people, she plucked a champagne flute off the tray of a passing waiter. Common sense advised the sparkling wine wouldn't beat back her encroaching headache, but it would make persevering through this evening a hell of a lot easier. The constant ingratiation, the dagger-wrapped-in-silk comments, the ever careful treading of shark-infested social waters—her mother was a gold medalist swimmer. But Sydney?

Too little patience, too thin skin, and too short a bullshit meter made her dead weight in the society maven pool.

Much to Charlene Blake's disappointment.

Glancing down at her slim, simple gold watch, she noted the time—nine fifteen p.m. The doors of the youth center would have been bolted fifteen minutes ago for the lock-in.

She smiled.

Yolanda and Melinda Evans, the no-nonsense sisters who ran the Maya Angelou Girls' Youth Center in Brighton, would have their hands full tonight and tomorrow morning with the twenty twelve- to fourteen-year-old girls expected to attend the sleepover. A heavy bank of wistfulness rolled through her. She should be there with the sisters and the teens. She'd been just as excited about the lock-in as the children who were her heart, her passion. They accepted and loved her unconditionally. They didn't see Sydney, the pampered socialite daughter of Jason Blake. They didn't see an unlimited bank account, an entrance into Boston society, or a wormhole into her father's good graces…or business deals. The girls at the center saw *her*. Sydney, who helped with their homework and offered them a listening ear and nonjudgmental heart. Sydney, who wasn't afraid to get sweaty in a game of kickball or join an impromptu *Just Dance 4* competition. Sydney, who told them how beautiful they were and believed every one of them was destined for greatness.

But while her volunteer work mentoring teens was ful-filling to her, to her parents, it didn't compare to organizing a tea, sitting on the beautification committee…or purchasing a bachelor. And when duty called—or rather, her parents' duties called—Sydney was required to answer.

The noose of family loyalty, obligations, and responsibility tightened around her throat, and she sipped from her glass, hoping to ease the rope burn.

With a sigh, she lowered to her satin-upholstered seat, her parents appearing moments later.

Applause erupted, and the level of animated conversation rose as the night's MC stepped up to the microphone once more. Somehow she doubted the enthusiasm was due to iPads in classrooms.

"Without further ado, let's bring on the bachelors!" the woman proclaimed. Moments later, a tall, slim man in an immaculate black tuxedo sauntered onto the stage. Even though a white mask hid his face from hairline to chin, he oozed confidence from every pore. Not that his self-assured-ness was a surprise. Though she didn't recognize him, she assumed he was most likely very aware of his desirability to the women packed into the room—after all, a requirement of every bachelor was at least a six-figure income.

Cynicism, thy name is Sydney.

"Our first bachelor of the evening may call Boston home, but the world is his office. As a financier, he's visited the white sands of Dubai, the wild cliffs of western Ireland, and the old-world beauty of his favorite city, Rome. The three adjectives that best describe him are driven, stubborn, and wildly romantic."

Appreciative laughter rippled through the crowd. The MC smiled and continued reading off her card. "Though he's never married, the woman he falls for will be spontaneous, independent, and have a wicked sense of humor. The woman who snags him tonight will enjoy dinner on a rooftop… in Rome." She waited for the exclamations to abate to a dull roar before continuing. "Dinner will be followed by a midnight walk in one of the city's famous squares and a shopping spree the next day before flying back home. Doesn't this sound divine? Let's open the bidding at twenty thousand." She nodded, beaming as she pointed at someone on the floor. "We have twenty thousand. What about twenty-one? Twenty-one. Twenty-two?"

And so the furious bidding began. Many paddle flicks later, bachelor number one went for seventy thousand dollars to a woman old enough to be his grandmother. *For his sake, please let her have bought him for her granddaughter, or even her daughter. Otherwise…* Sydney shuddered.

Bachelors two and three raised thirty and forty thousand dollars, respectively—they didn't offer dinner reservations in Italy—and as number four strolled off the stage after going for a respectable fifty thousand, Sydney zoned back in.

Tyler was bachelor number five. And in case she'd somehow forgotten, her mother's tap on her thigh was a not-so-subtle reminder.

"And bachelor number five," the hostess announced seconds before Tyler emerged from the wing. He strode out to the center of the stage and paused, his hands in the pockets of his tuxedo slacks. The stance accentuated the flatness of his stomach and the width of his chest. Maybe it was the spotlight or maybe that he stood on the wide stage alone with nothing to detract from him, but his six-foot frame seemed taller somehow. Under the stark black jacket his shoulders appeared wider…more powerful.

She shifted her gaze to his masked face. Tyler Reinhold was a handsome man, with his elegant, patrician features. Yet in the year they'd been dating, he'd never incited this vulnerable flicker of heat that danced in her belly like a candle's flame. His kisses and his touch were pleasant. But the knot currently twisting her gut could not be labeled…pleasant. Uncomfortable. Confusing. Hot.

But no, not pleasant.

A sliver of panic slipped under her ribs like the pointy tip of a stiletto. *No.* She was comfortable with their relationship. Comfortable with camaraderie rather than passion. She glanced in the mirror every morning—she was very much aware she could never be called a stunning beauty. Very much aware her family name and connections were as much a lure as her passably pretty looks. Most unions in their circle were more merger than marriage, anyway. And she preferred the cold but companionable alliance.

Especially since she could too vividly recall her mother's devastation after discovering affair after affair, until she'd finally evolved into a living mannequin who'd caulked off her heart against her husband's blatant infidelities.

No passion. No expectation of a grand, fiery love.

No pain.

For an insane moment, Sydney considered hiding the bidding paddle under her chair.

"Two little-known facts about bachelor number five are he played center on his high school basketball team and was cast as Bill Sikes in the drama club's production of *Oliver!*"

A wave of laughter followed the revelation, and it earned a chuckle from Sydney. Hmm. She hadn't known those surprising—and oddly charming details—about Tyler. "Eventually, he discovered he was much more coordinated and talented in the boardroom rather than on the court or stage. The woman who eventually becomes his leading lady will be intelligent, confident, and able to go toe-to-toe with him. Particularly since he considers his worst trait to be stubbornness. The lucky lady who ends up on the arm of this bachelor will hop a helicopter ride from Boston to New York, enjoying a Broadway production of Andrew Lloyd Webber's *Phantom of the Opera* and a late dinner at a five-star restaurant on the waterfront. Opening bid at ten thousand?"

Funny how she'd learned more intimate details about him in a two-minute spiel than she had in the year they'd been dating. She loved plays, particularly musicals, and had had no idea her fiancé shared the same appreciation. There went that small pool of disturbing warmth again. Shaking it off, she lifted her paddle.

The bidding war didn't last long. She won him at a suitable fifteen thousand with remarkable ease, almost as if the other women in the room realized who stood behind the mask as well. Silently, she huffed a sigh. *Who am I kidding?* They were probably very aware of Tyler's identity and made the prudent decision not to go up against Charlene Blake's formidable will.

Duty completed, Sydney barely paid attention to the rest of the auction. The evening flew by, and before long, the MC had called all the men back out onto the stage. They filed out in a straight line according to the order they'd appeared.

Sydney straightened in her seat, inexplicably eager to

see Tyler's face. A tiny voice whispered that this sudden, unbidden fascination with her fiancé was unwise…dangerous. Personal experience had taught her the Blake family fortune, reputation, and connections presented more of an allure than she did. "Plain" had been one boyfriend's description of her that she'd accidently overheard—much to his chagrin and disappointment when shortly thereafter he became her ex-boyfriend. But her father's position as CEO of the Blake Corporation? Very attractive.

Since then, she'd viewed relationships with a pragmatic eye. She entered in acknowledging they would be based on logic rather than love. A merger rather than a marriage. That's what she and Tyler had, and she welcomed it.

Still, she leaned forward, her entire focus aimed at bachelor number five.

"Now, what you've all been waiting for…" A drum roll vibrated on the air. "Bachelors, please remove your masks!"

As if time slowed to half speed, he removed the disguise. Inch by inch he revealed his strong jaw and chin. The full mouth. The strong jut of his cheekbones…

He pulled the mask free.

The air punched from her lungs, leaving her light-headed. The room spun around her, and for a horrifying moment, she almost pitched forward. At the last second, she gripped the edge of the table, steadying herself and preventing a humiliating tumble out of her chair.

The face carved out of stone that accentuated the carnal curve of the mouth…the dark slashes of eyebrows…the stunning turquoise eyes… They fit like puzzle pieces to form a truly beautiful man.

A man she'd never seen before.

Chapter Three

Round one: Lucas Oliver.

Triumph and satisfaction burned in his chest like a blazing torch as he studied the sudden burst of activity at the table directly in front of the stage. Jason and Charlene Blake leaned toward their daughter, their faces drawn into tight, furious lines. Sydney—the endgame in this evening's plan—wasn't looking at her parents, though. Didn't appear to be paying them any attention at all. Her focus was aimed at the stage. At him. The spotlight slightly blinded him to every nuance of her expression, but still…he felt her gaze on him. Like a light hand on his chest, his face. The touch was delicate, determined. Probing.

Inhaling sharply, he gave himself a mental shake, knocking aside the fanciful thought like an aggravating gnat.

"What the hell just happened?" a furious voice demanded next to him.

Arching an eyebrow, Lucas turned to the tall, dark-haired man to his left, a scowl lowering his eyebrows over his green glare. Tyler Reinhold, the fiancé of Sydney Blake. The man she'd assumed she was bidding on in the auction. But a promise to meet with the mistress of ceremonies' husband regarding a business proposal had garnered her cooperation in supplying the wrong information to Sydney.

Aiden would've called his tactics underhanded. Lucas preferred inventive.

"I'm sorry?" he replied to Tyler's hiss, feigning ignorance.

Tyler didn't reply but instead shot Lucas an eat-shit-and-die glance before storming off the stage. Lucas stared after the other man's retreating, stiff back then returned his gaze to the tableau unfolding on the floor. Sydney rose from the table, and her parents formed a barrier on either side of her. Though from his distance he couldn't catch the words, the tense figures, lowered heads, as well as the young woman's calm—too calm—expression telegraphed the verbal attack her parents waged.

And soon, her enraged fiancé would join the melee.

Damn. Turning sharply, he strode toward the wing and the exit at the bottom of the shadowed staircase. He didn't analyze or question the urgency in his steps or the need to act as her ally.

Even if that ally was a wolf in sheep's clothing.

Moments later, he approached the tight-knit group. He clenched his jaw, grinding his teeth together so hard he could've breathed enamel dust. With mother and father on either side of Sydney and fiancé in front, they looked like a legion of armies surrounding a fortified garrison.

Like she was the enemy.

"Excuse me," he murmured, smoothly aligning himself

next to her. "I'm sorry to interrupt." *Not a chance in hell.* "But I wanted to introduce myself." He smiled, clasping her hand in his and lifting it to his mouth. Ignoring her soft gasp and the dark scowls of the other three people, he brushed his lips over her knuckles and met a pair of lovely hazel eyes. He fought off a frown. Perhaps the loveliest he'd ever seen.

The alluring, fragile scent of honeysuckle wrapped around him. For a moment, her parents, fiancé, and even Lucas's own fifteen-year-old plans of revenge faded and disappeared into the netherworld outside the intimate circle enclosing him and Sydney Blake.

For six months now, Boston had been his temporary home, so he'd attended many of the same social events as she—had even glimpsed her tall, curvaceous figure and the long, straight fall of gold and brown hair—a vibrant, warm blend that couldn't be achieved or copied in a beauty salon.

Still, he'd never been this close, had never stood face-to-face with her. Had never detected the spattering of golden freckles dusting her nose and cheekbones that were barely discernible against her honeyed skin. Never glimpsed the sweet dip over her top lip that invited a man's tongue to sample, to taste. Never noted the sensual, plump fullness of a mouth created for sin and pleasure.

He'd never been near enough to notice the perfect indent of her waist, the beautiful thrust of her breasts against the emerald silk, or the sexy path of her hip. Thank God her mother—who resembled all the other thin-to-the-point-of-emaciated women in the room—hadn't managed to starve or shame the curves off her.

Slowly straightening, he lowered her hand and even more slowly released it. But he didn't liberate her from his scrutiny. The longer he stared, the more his perplexity grew. She wasn't the most beautiful woman he'd ever met. Since the age of sixteen, he'd dated—and fucked—many of them. Her mouth was a little too wide, her features just a shade too plain to be labeled beautiful. But the totality of her? The sensual promise in that imperfect but sexual mouth, the gorgeous almond-shaped eyes, the strong facial structure, and the walking-wet-dream body…she was alluring. She was tempting.

She was stunning.

"Lucas Oliver," Jason Blake greeted him, extending his hand, and though disgust curdled in his stomach, Lucas shook it. He ground his teeth together, silently ordering himself to smile but unable to manage it. When a man devoted his entire existence to greed and the relentless pursuit of more wealth, more assets, more power at the expense of loyalty, friendship, and honor, that evil should show on his face. Should etch his skin. Weather him. But God or fate seemed to favor the wicked. Because Jason Blake appeared as strong and handsome as he did in Lucas's memories. Though his closely shaven hair was liberally sprinkled with gray, lines barely etched his smooth, brown skin. His shoulders were wide and straight and the bright hazel eyes he'd bequeathed to his daughter were clear and sharp.

Lucas waited, bracing himself for any signs of recognition in the man's face. But aside from the polite smile, he didn't catch a flicker of acknowledgment from Jason. Then again, why should he recognize Lucas? The last time they'd encountered one another, Lucas had been a devastated, angry fifteen-year-old, and his last name had been Ellison. The son of Robert Ellison, Jason's former best friend and business partner, and the man he'd stepped on as carelessly as a pile of shit. Correction—Jason would've at least paused and wiped shit from the sole of his Italian loafer. He hadn't afforded Lucas's father the same courtesy.

"It's a pleasure to finally meet you face-to-face. I've heard so much about Bay Bridge Industries, all of it impressive," Jason boomed.

Giving the thieving bastard a nod and murmur of thanks that he nearly choked on, Lucas turned to the quiet woman he'd tricked into buying him.

"Since you've purchased me"—he flashed her a quick, disarming grin—"I figured I'd better get over here and introduce myself before you demanded a refund. Lucas Oliver."

"Nice to meet you," Sydney said, and the slight huskiness reminded him of a voice gone hoarse after hours of crying out in pleasure in the hottest, deepest part of night. His gut clenched in reaction. "Sydney Blake."

"I'm a little embarrassed, Mr. Oliver," Jason interrupted, stepping closer to his daughter. Too little, too late, but smart man. "I'd like to apologize on behalf of my daughter. I'm afraid there's been a misunderstanding—"

Lucas arched an eyebrow. "Really? I clearly remember Ms. Blake bidding on me. What is the confusion?"

Jason rolled his lips into a flat line, but Lucas read the unease in the gesture. *Good.* "Mr. Oliver, Sydney is engaged to Mr. Reinhold." He gestured behind him toward Tyler, who stood silent, his arms crossed. "He—"

"Congratulations," Lucas interjected smoothly.

Jason blinked, momentarily taken aback. "Well, yes, thank you. But you can see our dilemma."

Lucas cocked his head. "No, I can't."

The other man exhaled a hard, frustrated breath. "Somehow, she bid on the wrong man. My daughter believed you were her fiancé," he gritted out from between clenched teeth.

Now it was Lucas's turn to frown, but on the inside he delighted in Jason's discomfiture and irritation. *It won't be the last time you squirm for me, old man.*

"Of course with all of us being masked, you had to realize there was the chance this could happen?" Lucas paused, allowing a beat to pass between them, waiting to see if Jason would admit to knowing Tyler had been assigned a certain number. Or so they'd believed.

Jason didn't confess, but his angry silence spoke volumes. Shouted it. "Yes, we were aware—"

"Good," Lucas stated flatly. "Because when I agreed to participate in the auction, I made a commitment. One I intend to honor. And I'm sure the person who, in good faith, bid on Tyler expects him to do the same." Lucas turned to Sydney. "Ms. Blake, I'd like to discuss the arrangement with you about our evening." He held out his arm, and after a brief hesitation, she slid hers through his. "If you'll excuse us."

Not permitting Jason or Tyler an opportunity to object, he escorted her across the room. As they passed a waiter bearing a tray of champagne glasses, he collected two and pressed one into Sydney's free hand.

"I think you're going to need it by the time you return to your family," he said dryly, drawing a chair free of an empty table. Sydney didn't reply as she lowered to the seat, but she did sip from the flute. And the rim of the glass couldn't conceal the small smile curling her lips. Why the sight of that faint curve on her mouth warmed him, he couldn't explain. Maybe it was realizing her parents hadn't crushed the humor and life out of her yet. Lucas sat across from her.

"I'm sorry you had to walk into that, Mr. Oliver," she murmured. "My father means well, he just—"

"Doesn't want his daughter spending an evening with a stranger. More so when that daughter is engaged. He loves you. I understand." Not that he believed that bullshit for a second. Lucas grasped the reasons behind Jason's very vocal and enthusiastic support of his daughter's marriage to Tyler—or rather Tyler's family—even if Sydney didn't. Money, power, solidifying financial empires. Sydney's feelings or happiness probably hadn't been topping the list when her father considered the match. But familial love tended to blind a person to their loved one's true natures. "And it's Lucas."

Something dark flickered in her stare before her lashes lowered, preventing him from deciphering the flash of emotion. "Yes."

Nothing more. Just that simple, yet stark, yes. Again, the same surge of protectiveness reared its confusing head, the one that had driven him from the stage to join her in the stand against her family. He snuffed out the weak emotion before it had time to take root.

"What do you want, Sydney?" He dropped his voice, leaned forward. She blinked, almost as if surprised. As if not many people asked her that question. "I understand why your father objects, and honestly, I don't give a damn. But if you'd prefer not to go with me tomorrow night, then I'll accept your decision. From you. *For* you."

Not that he would accept a no. He'd come this far, was this close to seeing his plans coming to fruition, and he wouldn't allow her reluctance to stand in his way. But he sensed pressuring her wouldn't help him obtain his goal. Not after witnessing the interaction between her and her family. No, he had to take a soft approach with her, gain even a small amount of her trust. Rescuing her from the overbearing presence of her parents and Tyler had been the first step. Letting her think she had an option was another.

"I—" Her gaze shifted to somewhere over his shoulder, a tiny frown creasing her forehead.

"Look at me," he quietly ordered. With a soft gasp and almost imperceptible jerk of her head, she returned her regard to him. "It's your choice. Your desire. No one else's. I want to spend the evening with you, enjoying a Broadway play and getting to know you over dinner. I'd like you to want it, too. Yes or no, Sydney."

She stared at him, and for a moment, he wondered if he'd pushed too hard. Sydney was an unnerving dichotomy of vulnerability and strength, of sensuality and reserve. Even as she steadily met his eyes with barely there hints of uncertainty flashing in hers, he had no clue what she would decide.

His breath snagged in his throat as he waited for her reply. And he convinced himself it was because his plan hinged on the answer…not because he *wanted* her to *want* to spend time with him.

Fuck, he sounded like a girl. Next he would be writing notes asking her out and to check yes, no, or maybe.

"Yes or no, Sydney," he repeated, the need for her answer hardening his tone.

A beat of taut silence.

"Yes."

Chapter Four

"What the hell are you doing?" Sydney whispered to her reflection in the full-length cheval mirror the following evening. She smoothed slightly trembling hands over the waist and beaded belt of the floor-length black evening dress. After discarding five gowns, she'd settled on this one. The long sleeves and length were ideal for the October evening and an air-conditioned theater, while the beaded embellishments along the deep keyhole neckline prevented the dress from veering into Morticia territory. It said, *yes, I am on this date, but, no, I am not up for a one-night stand…or a visit to the morgue.*

Perfect.

Except for the nerves that ambushed her stomach.

She groaned, turning from her image before she found something else wrong—the color was drab, the material too formfitting, her hips looked too big, her ass was huge—and changed once more.

This was crazy. Had to be the most nonsensical thing she'd done in fourteen years. Again, what the hell was she thinking?

That's just it. She wasn't—she wasn't thinking.

For once, the opinions of her father, mother, Tyler, or others in their exclusive social circle didn't overshadow her own wants. For once, she wasn't censoring her own actions by someone else's guidelines and desires.

For once, she was doing what she wanted and to hell with the consequences.

Her belly twisted, belying the brave words marching through her head.

This was *so* not like her.

Even now, the fear of disappointing her parents and fiancé crept up her throat, threatening to strangle the breath from her lungs.

Don't. Hyperventilate.

Twenty-five years old and terrified of letting down her parents.

How pathetic would that sound to someone like Lucas Oliver, who didn't appear to be afraid of anyone or anything? She shivered as an image of the gorgeous, faintly intimidating business mogul filled her head. The tall, hard body he'd aligned next to hers as he faced down her parents and Tyler. The big, callused hands that had clasped her own. The midnight waves and loose curls that grazed his sharp cheekbones and granite jaw. The startling beauty of turquoise eyes that had bored into hers as he quietly, but firmly, ordered her to look at him.

Look at me.

The air stuttered in her throat but for a different reason

than fear. Those three words uttered in that dark, sensual voice had been like a caress over nerve endings she hadn't known existed. They had touched a place of yearning so deep inside her she'd obeyed the command before her brain comprehended and telegraphed the order. The need had been physical—good God, her panties could attest to that—but it'd also been emotional. He hadn't just been issuing an edict for her to return her gaze to him; he'd wanted to see her—her reaction, her wants, her thoughts…her. He'd wanted to see *her*.

Other than the Evans sisters and the young girls she mentored, Sydney couldn't remember the last time someone had wanted to just see *her*.

How could she not have said yes?

Damn, how *could* she have said yes?

A perfunctory knock on her bedroom door echoed seconds before her mother entered.

"I see you're still determined to go through with this… outing," she stated, her tone as tightly drawn as the thin line of her mouth. "Really, Sydney, I have no idea what you could be thinking."

That seemed to be the opinion of the day, didn't it?

"Mom, I already explained my decision to you and Dad."

"Yes, I know, you made a commitment. Fine. But you could have signed the check and passed on this date with an unknown"—she turned her lips up in a disgusted moue—"uncouth stranger. He's disfigured, for God's sake," she spat. "I can only imagine how *that* came about."

Of course she'd seen the scar. It was impossible to miss, since it bisected his obsidian eyebrow and continued in a thin ridge under his right eye. The scar appeared to be an old one, but the original wound must have been horrible to leave behind such a visible mark. But unlike her mother, Sydney didn't find it repulsive. No, the mark added to his dangerous, warrior-in-a-suit air. He reminded her of a barely domesticated panther: dark, sleek, muscled, beautiful, predatory. The Beast of Bay Bridge, she'd learned people called him. The nickname probably wasn't meant as flattery and referred to the name of his corporation and most likely his business reputation rather than his appearance. Regardless of the meaning behind the moniker, his masculine beauty invited a woman to touch, to pet, but at her own peril. Because this gorgeous animal did—and would—bite.

And from the information she'd read on the internet last night after arriving home, women petted often…and he allowed it. She'd scrolled through the images from the Boston society pages, and she'd never glimpsed the same woman on his arm twice. Still, his dates all seemed to have several things in common: supermodel beauty, skinny bodies, and big, happy smiles.

"He's a reputable and very successful businessman, not a criminal," she said, glancing at the clock on her bedside table. Four fifteen. Lucas should arrive in several minutes to pick her up. The play started at seven, and the helicopter ride would take about an hour and a half. "Besides, Dad knows him."

"Knows *about* him," Charlene corrected. "There's a difference. And believe me, your father is not pleased with this by any means." She paused, studied Sydney, and tapped a manicured fingertip against her bottom lip. "Do you think that's the wisest choice for a dress? It's not very…forgiving, is it?"

Heat blasted Sydney's face, and she struggled not to flinch or betray the hurt that was like a punch to the chest. After years of the same criticisms, careless remarks, and thinly veiled insults, she should be numb to the pain and humiliating reminders she wasn't a perfect size two or zero. Reminders she just wasn't…perfect. Maybe in another twenty years, she would grow the Teflon skin required to exist and thrive in her social set—and her family.

"I don't have time to change," Sydney replied, erasing all hints of emotion from her voice. All her mother needed was the slightest indication that she'd scored a hit in Sydney's armor, and Charlene would harp even more on Sydney's weight and appearance, calling it *motivation*. "Lucas should be here in a few minutes." She lowered to her bed and slipped her foot into her jewel-encrusted black shoe.

"Lucas," her mother repeated, sneering. Sydney didn't glance up from fastening the strap around her ankle. "Already you're so familiar. When did that happen? When you walked off with him last night? You embarrassed Tyler, which to a man like him is unforgivable. And now you're allowing him to go on a date with another woman? Foolish! You're just handing him over as if there are men like him lining up around the corner. Sydney." Charlene set a thin but strong palm on her shoulder. Molding her expression into a cool, detached mask, Sydney lifted her head and met her mother's scrutiny. "We only want the best for you…for all of us."

Her heart beat against her sternum like a caged animal, mirroring how she felt. Trapped. Imprisoned by duty, responsibility, and guilt. All of her life, she'd bowed to her father and mother's expectations: earning great grades, attending the college of their choice, living at home after graduation and assisting her mother with her varied charities and social events instead of getting a job and a place of her own…dating and becoming engaged to a man they approved of. A man to whom marriage was both a social and financial coup.

Not rocking the boat had become an ingrained habit. Because the one time she'd disobeyed her parents and hadn't listened to their order, it had resulted in catastrophic consequences, their lives forever altered.

The cost of her selfishness and defiance had been her little brother's life.

A soft rap on the door prevented—or saved—her from responding to her mother's pointed reminder of duty. And the memories.

"Come in," Sydney called out.

A moment later, their housekeeper opened the door and poked her head inside the room.

"Ms. Sydney, a Mr. Lucas Oliver has arrived for you."

"Thank you, Maddie." After the other woman left, Sydney retrieved her wide-collared coat from her closet and headed for the door.

"Sydney—"

"Everything will be fine, Mom." She grasped the knob before glancing over her shoulder with a small, reassuring smile. "It's just one night. There's no need to worry."

• • •

"Thank you," Sydney murmured as Lucas removed her coat and handed both of theirs to the New York restaurant's coat check. He placed a hand to the small of her back, and they followed the host as he led them to their table. A shiver threatened to dance over her skin and through her body, but she stifled it. There was nothing she could do about the palm-sized circle of heat radiating from her skin where Lucas touched her, though.

All night she'd been waging this particular battle. She'd thoroughly enjoyed the play; *Phantom of the Opera* was one of her favorites, and the historical Majestic Theatre had been opulent and beautiful. But her delight had been tempered by an almost painful awareness of him the entire time. Of his big body sitting next to her, making her feel—for the first time in her life—delicate and petite. His arm and knee had pressed against hers for two hours, and the firm, constant contact had competed with the timeless story of love, horror, and tragedy that unfolded on the stage.

The contrast in her overwhelming reaction to this man she'd known less than twenty-four hours to the man she planned to spend the rest of her life with should've been alarming. Lucas incited a riot of confusion, desire, and consciousness of her body with just his nearness that Tyler hadn't managed with an actual kiss. More than ever, she was aware of the life she intended to consign herself to—one of levelness and complacency. One without extreme highs or lows of emotions or needs…just a steady, even-keeled existence.

But instead of panicking her, the realization soothed her, ensured her she was making the correct choice with Tyler. Good God, if one evening with Lucas had her alternating between fascination, lust, uncertainty, and joy, then what would a relationship be like?

Exhausting.

And full of anxiety and insecurity. Images of the parade

of women from those articles leaped to her mind. Yes, there would be passion, but that desire would end up shackling her to a man who could never love her back the way she needed. A man who could never be faithful.

Why are you so quick to believe gossip columns, a small, insidious voice whispered inside her head.

A hint of shame wormed inside her chest. Especially since even she—with as boring an existence as she led—had been the target of thinly veiled jabs and gossip in the scandal rags and online tabloids. But, as unfair as choosing to believe the rumors about him was, she latched on to what she'd read. Chose to believe. Because that made him unsuitable to her, beyond her reach…safer.

No. Tyler—who didn't cause her heart to pound or the bottom to fall out of her stomach like a dizzying free fall down a roller coaster—was her ideal.

Perfect.

The host paused next to a table hidden from most of the room by a waist-high wall and tall, exotic plants. Private. Intimate. *Dangerous*, she silently added. The host moved to pull out her chair, but Lucas shifted forward, slid the high-backed chair from under the table, and waited for her to be seated. Just for a moment, he lingered behind her, and the back of his fingers grazed her shoulders. This time she couldn't stifle the shudder of pleasure his brief but indelible touch caused. And when he froze behind her for several more seconds, she wondered if he'd caught the telltale reaction.

Oh, yes, he had.

The answer reverberated inside her head when Lucas lowered to the chair across from her, his fierce gaze locked on her face. His scrutiny was neither polite nor impersonal but piercing, hooded…hot. Beneath her dress, her nipples beaded, the soft silk of her bra suddenly chafing and constricting. A sweet, nagging ache pulsed between her thighs, and she squeezed her thighs together, trying to alleviate the sensual torment. And succeeded in intensifying—worsening—it.

The timely arrival of their sommelier allowed her to inhale an inconspicuous breath, and while Lucas tasted the different wine offerings, she wrangled her body back into submission. Had she said dangerous? This man was positively lethal.

"Did you enjoy the play?" he asked, extending a glass containing a deep ruby wine toward her. "Taste?" Then watched, with piercing intensity, as she sipped. The rich but sweet bouquet of the cabernet smoothed over her tongue, and she lowered her lashes, humming slightly in appreciation. When she lifted them, the approval hovering on her lips died a swift death. His gaze was fixed on her mouth. Nervously, she swiped the tip of her tongue over her lips, and his expression hardened, the carnality more pronounced. The scar over and under his eye only emphasized the danger inherent in the stare. No man had ever looked at her with such…hunger. As if he was seconds from jerking her to her feet and crashing his mouth to hers and feasting like a starved man.

She gasped, and the hooded turquoise scrutiny lifted, the heat there bright…scalding.

"Do you like it?" The question referred to the wine, but the low, rough timbre of his voice hinted at something else—something civilized people didn't discuss over a linen-covered table at a five-star restaurant in a room full of people.

"Yes," she whispered, settling the glass on the table with trembling hands before folding them in her lap. "It's delicious."

"Good." He nodded and ordered a bottle from the silent sommelier.

Oh my God. She swallowed a groan. How could she have forgotten about the other man's presence? Heat prickled her skin. What kind of magic did Lucas Oliver wield to capture her mind and senses so completely?

"So," he continued, "the play. Did you enjoy it?"

Right. The play. "I did," she replied, and thanked God for small favors that her voice didn't wobble. "I love *Phantom of the Opera*. The story, the romance, the music." She laughed softly. "I have to admit, musicals are one of my vices."

"Just one?" A corner of his mouth quirked. "So just how many do you have?"

"Enough that they require more than one bottle of wine to confess to," she retorted, arching an eyebrow. His dark, sexy chuckle necessitated another sip of her drink. At this rate, she might be spilling all her secrets by the time dessert was served. "Do you have a favorite play?"

"Several. *Phantom of the Opera. Les Misérables. Chicago.*" He smiled, and she returned the gesture, knowing from her online research that he'd grown up in the Windy City. His company's headquarters were still stationed there. "And," he paused, "*Lion King.*"

She grinned. "*Simba, you have forgotten me.*" She dragged out her best James-Earl-Jones-as-Mufasa impression, and Lucas laughed, humor transforming him from beautiful to beautiful squared. "*Lion King* was wonderful. I also loved *Wicked.* And of course *Grease.*"

"Of course," he drawled. "But if you're waiting for me to bust out a verse of 'Summer Nights,' it's going to be a long night."

"Damn." She snapped her fingers, shaking her head. Lucas snorted, lifting his glass to his mouth. The wide globe appeared fragile in his long-fingered grip. Quickly diverting her attention, she asked, "So was the bit in your introduction at the auction true? Did you really play Bill Sikes in your high school musical?"

His lips twisted, the expression self-deprecating. "I'm afraid so. But not out of any great love for the theater or *Oliver!* That was just a happy, but unintentional, result. See, Colleen Moore had tried out for the role of Nancy. I figured if we were both in the play, we would spend a lot of after-noons and nights together at rehearsals, never considering she had the singing voice of a cat in heat." Sydney choked out a laugh, and he shrugged. "Unfortunate, but very true. Mine wasn't that much better, but I could hold a note and memorize a script. Besides"—the smile he wore turned a shade more sinister as he tapped the end of his scar—"I had the rough, criminal look down."

"Does it bother you?" she murmured, the question slip-ping from her lips before she could think better of asking it. The mark appeared too old to cause him pain, but she hadn't been referring to the physical. She bit the inside of her cheek. She'd been too bold; they were here for a light dinner before parting and probably never seeing each other again except for the occasional social event. Did she hon-estly expect him to spill his deepest emotions?

"Does it bother *you*?" he countered softly.

Bother her? Yes. Her heart ached when she thought of

the suffering he must've endured. During and after. From experience, she knew people weren't…kind to those they perceived as different. Any imperfection was pointed out, jeered at, or lamented over. Maybe some of those same people were responsible for dubbing him the Beast. Oh, yes. That bothered her, since he'd been nothing but lovely and considerate to her since their first meeting.

But did the scar detract from his appearance? No—hell, no. It added to his masculine beauty, lent it an element of danger that was both alarming and seductive.

Yet if she admitted the truth, he would think she was either desperate or needy. So she settled for, "Not at all. Why should it?"

An emotion flashed in his eyes before he smirked and leaned back in his chair. He didn't respond but turned the conversation to more mundane territory. Regret flickered in her chest. Why did she feel as if she'd failed some test? She buried the pang of hurt and answered his questions about Boston, family, and herself. Which was novel. Most of her and Tyler's exchanges revolved around him, his family's company, or whatever party or benefit they planned to attend.

The hour sped by, and when their waiter set a cup of after-dinner coffee in front of her, she realized their date was nearing an end. Squelching the disappointment, she added cream to the dark brew.

"How long have you and Tyler Reinhold been engaged?"

Surprised, she glanced up, the spoon she'd been stirring with still clasped in her fingers. "Not long," she said, silently scolding herself. She should have no problem talking about her fiancé. This was an outing because of an *auction*, not a regular date. Lucas wasn't enamored with her, no matter what her overactive imagination might have conjured. She cleared her throat. "We've been together for a year, though."

"He seems very protective of you. Not that I can blame him. Auction or not, if you were mine, I wouldn't have let you fly to another city with a man who wasn't me."

If you were mine. She highly doubted he'd claimed any woman as *his.* That would be too permanent. "I don't belong to him like a piece of real estate with a deed," she snapped. And immediately hated the display of irritation. Because the description pretty much summed up her arrangement with Tyler. Theirs wasn't a love match; they were an amicable, companionable merger. And she preferred it that way… damn it.

A small smile played across his sensual mouth. "You don't like the idea of belonging to a man, Sydney? The idea of knowing beyond a doubt that he's claimed you so thoroughly, your body's marked by him, your blood heats for him and him alone? The idea that you're his, and if any man even looks in your direction, he's taking his life into his own hands?"

"No," she breathed. She didn't. He described everything she was afraid of—blind passion, possession, jealousy. So why did the heat pouring through her like a stream of lava brand her a liar? "Would you want that with a woman? You don't seem like the kind of man who would appreciate or tolerate a jealous, possessive woman."

He arched an eyebrow. "I wouldn't. And I agree with you. I don't want what I just mentioned. I prefer a relationship of respect with someone who is independent, has her own interests. Someone who understands I don't work a nine-to-five and is content with that. Desire is easy—lust easier. More than a lover, I want a woman who can hold her own in a social situation or a boardroom as well as the bedroom."

"And love? I noticed love wasn't included on your list."

"No," he said flatly, something too fleeting and shadowed to decipher flashing in his eyes. "It wasn't. Which brings me to my next question, Sydney."

He leaned back in his chair and steepled his fingers under chin. His intense gaze ensnared her, refused to free her, even though she desperately wanted to avoid the piercing scrutiny. The conversation had left her off-kilter, his cold, matter-of-fact analysis of his desired relationship unsettling. Even though he'd echoed what she and Tyler had. What she was pledging her life to as Mrs. Reinhold.

She reached for her coffee, desperate for a distraction from him…from her own thoughts.

"Yes? What is it?"

"Marry me."

It wasn't a question.

Chapter Five

Fraud. Jail. Marry me.

The words whirled in Sydney's head like a demonic merry-go-round as she strode into the lobby of the building housing the headquarters of the Blake Corporation the next morning. With a quick nod at the security guard, she continued at a fast clip to the bank of elevators. As if by walking faster she could outdistance the memories of the previous evening and Lucas Oliver's accusations and threats. Outrun the anger and fear that congealed in her stomach, souring it. She huffed out a breath. Not damn possible.

God, she felt like such a fool allowing herself to be charmed by his attentiveness, by the sensuality that emanated off him like steam off a sidewalk after a quick summer shower. Like a lamb led to slaughter—was that what he'd been thinking as he'd escorted her to the play and dinner? Right before he blindsided her with a proposal of marriage?

Not that he'd been shocked or offended by her quick,

and harsh, "Go to hell." Not Lucas Oliver. A quirk of the corner of his mouth had been his reaction as he handed her a folder—and proceeded to blackmail her. Her hand in marriage to prevent the loss of her father's reputation and company. A devil's bargain from a devil.

Or a beast.

She punched the up button on the panel, and seconds later, the metal doors hissed open. The twenty-second ride to the top floor of the steel and glass building seemed like twenty years before she emerged from the elevator into the hallway leading to her family's corporate offices. A foreign urgency vibrated under her skin, almost as if a hand at her back propelled her down the corridor to the office waiting at the end. She nodded and murmured subdued hellos to the employees who greeted her, but she didn't pause to chat as she usually would have. The need for answers trumped manners or politeness. The need to affirm that her world didn't teeter on the crumbling edge of uncertainty and lies.

The need to verify she hadn't become the pawn in a very real and threatening game of blackmail.

"Good morning, Sydney," Cheryl Granger said with a wide smile as Sydney paused in front of the desk where the CFO's executive assistant sat. As long as she could remember, the stately woman had stood guard behind her wide desk, answering phones, typing reports, welcoming those with appointments, and turning away those without. Though Cheryl's hair bore more gray than brown now, she was a fixture in the Blake Corporation offices. And one of Sydney's favorite people.

"Hi, Cheryl." She forced a smile to her lips. "Is he in?"

The receptionist frowned, apparently not fooled by

Sydney's caricature of a smile. "For you? Always." She rose
from her chair and headed toward the closed oak door behind her. With a perfunctory knock, she opened the door
and stuck her head inside. "Mr. Henley, Sydney is here to see
you." Cheryl stepped back and waved Sydney inside.

"Thanks, Cheryl," she whispered before entering Terry
Henley's inner sanctum. The dam she'd been hoarding her
emotions behind creaked and groaned as her godfather
stood and rounded his massive glass desk, wearing a wide
grin and with his arms outstretched.

"Sydney." He enfolded her in his embrace, and the familiar scents of imported cigars and cologne wrapped around
her as securely as his arms. Fissures zigzagged across the
dam now, springing leaks. Terry was not only the chief financial officer of the Blake Corporation but also her father's
oldest friend. He'd been a fixture in her life—a dependable,
loving fixture. Where Jason had been miserly with affection,
Terry had been generous. Where Jason had been absent, Terry had been available. Where Jason had been cold, distant,
Terry had been warm…forgiving.

In many respects, Terry had been the father Jason hadn't
been—refused to be.

And this morning when she'd thrown back the blankets,
Lucas's unbelievable and detestable charges driving her
from the bed, her first thought had been to run to Terry, not
Jason. Even though Lucas's claims had been laid against her
father.

Fraudulent financial statements. Submitting false IRS
reports. And if she didn't marry Lucas, he would ruin Jason.
And Lucas's reason for carrying out his blackmail scheme?
He would only say that he hated her father. So simple, yet she

had no doubt it was so very complicated. Jason couldn't have risen to be the powerful man he was today without earning his fair share of enemies. And considering his penchant for other women besides his wife, that number could be even greater.

"What did I do to warrant this pleasure?" Terry squeezed her close once more before cupping her shoulders and leaning back. Again, she tried to smile, to shore up her admittedly weak defenses, but like Cheryl, he saw straight through the facade. His smile faltered then disappeared, his bushy gray eyebrows arrowing down. "Sydney? What's wrong?"

She pinched the bridge of her nose, dipped her chin. How did she ask this? How did she even form her lips around the question hovering on her tongue? Not by any stretch of the imagination did Jason win father of the year. But he was still her father.

And at one time he'd been tender, doting. Before Jay… before they'd lost Jay, he'd been the parent little girls dreamed and bragged about. Her little brother's death—and her role in it—had transformed him into the detached, critical, aloof man he was today. She'd done that. Her negligence and impetuousness had done that. So how did she dare question his integrity? How did she dare question…anything?

"Sydney?" Terry murmured, guiding her to the brown leather sofa in his sitting area. Gently, he lowered her to the cushion, sitting beside her and cradling her hands between his. "Talk to me. Tell me what's bothering you."

She inhaled a shuddering breath, slowly exhaled it.

"Terry." She lifted her head and met the concern in his gray eyes. "Is Dad—" She hesitated. Hating herself. "Is Dad…in trouble?"

Her godfather's frown deepened. "What do you mean?"

"Is he—the company—in financial trouble? Has he been lying"—the word tasted sour on her tongue, and she barely managed not to choke on it—"to banks and investors to keep the business afloat?" Lucas had used the term "cooking the books." She might have majored in psychology instead of business, but she understood the ugliness of the accusation.

A shutter seemed to slam shut in Terry's gaze, wiping his face clean of expression, leaving a blank, impassive mask. "Where did you hear this from, Sydney?"

Not an indignant "No, of course not," or even a dismissive "Don't believe everything you hear." Her heart pounded against her chest like a jackhammer, thundering in her ears.

"Does it matter?" she asked woodenly. "Is it true? And please don't lie to me." *I can't—Dad can't—afford for you to lie to me.*

Terry didn't respond for several long moments, just studied her in the heavy silence suddenly filled with a tension that crawled over her skin.

"I need to know where you came by this rumor," he eventually stated, the godfather she loved replaced by the Blake Corporation's chief financial officer.

"I can't reveal that." When he parted his lips, she repeated the gesture, only harder, her refusal adamant. "Trust me when I say I can't. But I need to know. Please," she quietly begged. Slipping her hands free of his, she reversed the hold so her palms enfolded his. "Please, Terry."

His piercing scrutiny thawed the slightest bit. "Sydney, as CFO…"

"You're bound by confidentiality. I know. But I wouldn't

ask if it weren't important. And I can't go to Dad with this. I can't — " She squeezed his hands. "Please," she repeated.

Another stretch of time passed before his lashes lowered, and he shot from the couch. He shoved a hand through his thick silver strands, and her stomach plummeted toward her feet. Panic clawed at her throat as the uncharacteristic agitated gesture confirmed her fears. Lucas's accusations.

"Oh, God, Terry," she breathed.

He whirled around, pinned her to the couch with a narrowed stare. "Tell me what you've heard."

She jerked her head in an unsteady nod. "Blake Corporation has been in financial trouble for the last five years. And for the last three, Dad has been overreporting the company's income and assets then using the inflated earning reports to drive up the stock price and acquire fraudulent bank loans and new investors on falsified information." She opened her purse and removed a thin folder containing a detailed accounting of Lucas's claims. He'd given it to her last night as she'd exited the limousine, instructing her to read it. Most of the columns of numbers, dates, and names had been an undecipherable jumble to her, but the typed report had been clear and concise. Hand trembling, she extended the file to Terry.

He accepted it and returned to his desk. After a while, he stood, the incriminating folder still clutched in his hand. Instead of addressing her, though, he turned to the wall of glass behind him that offered a gorgeous view of the Charles River. But from the tense line of his jaw and unyielding set of his shoulders, she doubted he was appreciating the sea of steel, glass, and brick.

"Whomever you spoke with seems to have a lot of

insider information."

Abandoning her perch on the couch, she crossed the room, pausing at his side.

"So it's true," she whispered.

"Yes," he said.

The single-word confirmation seemed to resound like a death knell. A fist-sized knot banded around her lungs until bare wisps of air escaped her lips.

"Why?" The question was barely a sigh of sound, but Terry caught it. He shook his head, his gaze still trained on the window.

"There are reasons—reasons that seemed valid and logical at the onset. But do they matter now? Whatever the original intentions—reputation, job employment, tradition, profit—the result is the same. We're in over our heads. Have been for a while. Jason hopes your marriage to Tyler will—" He broke off the explanation and flinched, realizing what he'd been about to reveal. Pain flickered across his handsome, suddenly weary features, and she shifted closer, grasping his hand. The ache in her chest was negligible. Of course she'd understood from the beginning why her father had been elated over her relationship with Tyler. Two dominant financial institutions allied through marriage. But now her father's enthusiasm was cast in a whole new light—the light of desperation. "Anyway, with the backing and impeccable reputation of the Reinhold Corporation, he hopes to infuse new capital into the company, covering the discrepancies before they can be discovered."

She swallowed, trying to moisten her suddenly dry mouth. "And if not?" she rasped.

"If not, then the company will eventually be investigated

by the SEC, and your father, myself, and other individuals will face federal charges." His gaze narrowed, sharpened. "Why? Did something happen between you and Tyler?"

She shook her head. Her and Tyler? No. "We're fine. I just wanted the entire picture."

"Sydney." He turned, gathered her close. "This is our mess. *Ours*. We realized the potential consequences when we started this course. Regardless of your father's expectations or wishes, it's not fair to expect you to marry someone to save us from our mistakes. What I'm saying is if you don't"—he hesitated before continuing—"love Tyler the way a woman should when pledging her life and heart to a man, then you shouldn't. I know your father can be intimidating, and the pressure he places on you isn't fair. But if you have any misgivings…"

She didn't reply—couldn't. Love, despair, and resignation trapped the words. Words that would've been lies anyway. *I love Tyler. Tyler loves me.* As much as Terry cared for her, had striven to protect and give her the affection her parents should have offered, she couldn't grasp the avenue of escape he offered.

Loyalty.

Duty.

Sacrifice.

Those three virtues had been drummed into her head from birth. Her wants and needs finished a distant second to the family's. Especially for Sydney, who had selfishly cost the family so much.

Her brother, Jason Raymond Blake II—Jay, for short—had been born when Sydney was six. As the long-awaited son, he'd been doted on by their parents from the beginning.

And one mistake, one act of defiance and negligence on ten-year-old Sydney's part had led to his drowning in the family pool. Four years old. He'd lost his life at the precious age of four.

And it'd been her fault—his death had been her fault. If she hadn't disobeyed her parents and left the back door ajar for him to escape through, Jay wouldn't have jumped in the unattended pool and died. Her father had said as much.

Though fifteen years had passed since that tragic day, her family still suffered the loss. They never spoke of Jay, as if he hadn't ever existed. His pictures didn't decorate the walls or mantel in the living room along with those of the rest of the family. And though Jason had gruffly apologized to her for his grief-stricken accusations after the tragedy had occurred, the truth and guilt still weighed down her soul like the heaviest albatross.

Her selfish disobedience had stolen his son. Now, years later, she couldn't allow her own desires to cost him the company to which he'd dedicated over half his life.

No. She'd marry and save her father. Just not Tyler.

It was the very least she could do.

"Thank you for telling me, Terry," she murmured. Rising on her toes, she kissed his cheek. "I have to meet Mom for brunch, so I need to go."

"Okay." Giving her one last squeeze, he loosened his embrace, allowing her to step back. "Tell Charlene I said hello."

"I will." But she wouldn't. Then her mother would ask why she'd visited Terry in the first place. Better to avoid that inquisition. "I'll call you later."

Minutes later, she stood on the sidewalk outside the

office building, her conversation with her godfather playing on an endless loop through her mind. Blindly, she stared ahead, not seeing the busy morning traffic or hearing the cacophony of drills and raised voices from the ongoing construction across the street.

She exhaled slowly.

She had no choice.

Removing her cell from her purse, she gripped it tight before retrieving the heavy, cream-colored business card embossed with royal-blue ink. Flipping it over, she studied the ten digits with a Chicago area code, then before she could lose the sliver of courage she still retained, punched in the cell phone number.

The other end rang once. Twice.

Then the dark, sensual voice that had tormented her dreams the previous night rumbled in her ear.

"Mr. Oliver," she said. "This is Sydney Blake. We need to talk. I'll be at your office in half an hour."

Chapter Six

"Mr. Oliver, Ms. Blake is here to see you," his executive assistant informed him.

Lucas pressed the speaker button on the multiline desk phone. "Please send her in," he ordered, rising from his office chair. Grim satisfaction and more than a little bit of anticipation coursed through him, headier than the most potent alcohol. He studied the closed door, a hot heaviness settling in his gut. He could try to convince himself he watched the entrance like an eagle sighting prey because he wanted to grab hold of this triumphant moment. To savor it. But he wasn't in the habit of lying to himself.

And the pounding in his cock didn't give a damn about revenge.

"Ms. Blake? Sydney Blake?" Aiden asked, standing from his perch on the corner of Lucas's desk.

Lucas flicked a glance in his best friend's direction before returning his attention to the office door. "Yes. Sydney

Blake."

"Son of a…" Aiden glared at him, disapproval emanating off him. "I thought you said she told you to go to hell."

He shrugged. "She did. But that wasn't a no."

Aiden growled, dragging a hand through his hair. "You've got to be fucking kidding me. You can't go through with this, Luke." His eyes flashed with a disappointment that cut Lucas like a shard of glass. "This is crazy. I've seen you make some insane decisions that somehow panned out in the end. But that was business. This is…" He spread his hands wide, palms up as if in supplication to a conscience Lucas didn't possess when it came to Jason Blake. "This is her life. *Your* life. Rethink this. Please."

The door to his office cracked open, and his assistant stepped in. But he didn't see her. He forgot about Aiden and his pleas as every bit of his awareness zeroed in on the tall, regal woman gliding into the room. He devoured every detail of her appearance—from the long ponytail that swayed against the middle of her straight spine as she thanked his receptionist to the thrust of high, generous breasts under the simple but elegant wrap dress.

With a bite of cynicism, he swept his gaze over the sensual swell of her hips. She probably detested their roundness, as most of the women he knew craved to own the body of a prepubescent child rather than a grown, real woman. His uncle, the man who'd raised him after his father's death, had a saying: "Only dogs want bones. And they bury them." He and Uncle Duncan had disagreed on many subjects, but this one thing—the beauty of a woman's curves—wasn't one of them. Staring at Sydney's small waist, full hips, and firm ass, he didn't see fat.

He saw his fingers digging into her flesh, holding her still for a wild, raw fucking that would leave them sweaty, sore, and wrecked. He saw a gorgeous, sexy body that could take the fierceness, the roughness, the untamed lust he often had to leash with his sex partners. With those soft thighs wrapped around his hips, she would take every bit of his cock, every hard thrust.

He'd even let her keep those sexy-as-hell knee-high black boots on.

"Oh." She drew up short as she noticed Aiden. "I'm sorry. I didn't know you were busy."

"We're not," he said shortly. "He's leaving."

Aiden scowled at Lucas, muttering under his breath. Lucas caught "dumb" and "ass" before his friend turned and extended his hand toward Sydney with a warm smile. "Please forgive him his manners. They left for lunch some years ago, and unfortunately, we're still looking for them," he drawled. "I'm Aiden Kent, COO of Bay Bridges and his"—he jerked his head in Lucas's direction—"best friend. My canonization for sainthood should be coming through any day now."

She chuckled. "Sydney Blake."

"Don't you have a meeting to attend?" Lucas snapped, not as irritated by his friend's sarcasm as by the sight of Sydney's smile at Aiden's humor.

With a dramatic sigh, Aiden released Sydney's hand. "I suppose I do. Nice meeting you, Ms. Blake." He stalked across the room but not before pinning Lucas with one last glare as he shut the door behind him.

Sydney faced him, all traces of amusement ebbing from her lovely features until a polite mask remained.

"Mr. Oliver. Thank you for agreeing to see me on such

short notice."

The husky, sensuous timbre so at odds with the cool reserve was a temptation in itself. The contradiction taunted him. He wondered which epitomized the true woman—the sex-and-sin voice or the aloof society princess aura.

Damn, he wanted—*needed*—to peel back the layers and uncover the reality for himself.

"Lucas," he smoothly corrected, but with a hint of steel. The previous night—before he'd blackmailed her on the back of a marriage proposal—he'd been Lucas to her. She might consider him an adversary now, but hell if he'd allow her to lodge this particular barrier between them. Some people said pick your battles... Screw that. Win every one of them, and no one will have to worry about who won the war. Because he would be the only one left standing. "Considering the circumstances, formality is a little ridiculous."

Other than the slight tightening of her mouth, she didn't display a reaction. He rounded the desk and approached her, pausing only when mere inches separated them. The combination of honeysuckle and skin teased him, urged him to bury his face in the soft crook between her neck and shoulder and inhale. The sweet scent probably came from something as mundane as lotion. Still, he couldn't help but wonder if that tantalizing aroma would be thicker, richer in the hidden places. The shadowed valley between her breasts. The sensitive, tender skin behind her knee. Between her thighs. He fisted his fingers. Yeah, it would definitely be stronger and more intoxicating near the pretty, swollen folds of her sex.

"Why are you here, Sydney?" he murmured, deliberately using her given name. He shifted closer, invading even more of her space. Curious to see what she would do. And was surprised when she didn't retreat. Admiration curled in his chest. Not many people dared to stare down the Beast of Bay Bridge.

"You know why I'm here," she replied, her attention trained on some distant point over his shoulder. "To discuss the…arrangement you proposed last night."

He slid his hands in the front pockets of his slacks. "Look at me when you speak to me, Sydney," he ordered softly. She obeyed, and the anger her aloof manner and careful voice hid so well blazed at him from her hazel stare. "Now. What about it?"

A humorless smile lifted the corner of her mouth. "You're going to make me beg, is that it?"

"Beg?" Slowly, he shook his head. "No, that's not my intention." He paused, his scrutiny briefly dipping to her mouth. "At least not here."

He caught her low gasp as the implication behind his words sank deep, and she shifted back a step. Hmm. His physical presence hadn't made her retreat, but a sexual innuendo did.

Interesting.

Maybe she realized her error in allowing him to witness her discomfort, because she hurriedly recovered the space she'd placed between them. But it was a little too late for that. He'd seen the chink in her armor. And like any good businessman, he intended to take advantage of it.

He smiled.

The small catch in her breath didn't escape his notice. Neither did the flutter of her pulse in the shallow bowl at the base of her throat.

"You asked me to marry you," she murmured.

"Yes."

"If the offer is still open, I'd like to talk about the terms."

After a long, heavy moment, he nodded and gestured toward one of the two visitor chairs flanking the front of his desk. Sydney lowered to the seat with the grace of a queen, her spine ramrod straight, shoulders back, chin tilted up. The perfect socialite. The perfect lady.

Aiden would've caustically added, "The perfect sacrifice."

Maybe. And a shade of guilt might've tinged the victory bubbling in his blood. But he smothered it. There were always wounded and collateral damage in battle—hell, he should know. He'd been a casualty in the cowardly ambush Jason Blake waged on Lucas's father.

In this war between Jason and Lucas, Sydney was an unfortunate, but necessary, martyr.

After moving to perch on the edge of the desk, he crossed his arms, his legs spread wide, feet bracketing her chair. Caging her between the seat and his body.

"I made the terms clear last night," he said, voice flat. "Marry me, and keep your father out of jail and his business solvent for future Blake generations." He twisted his mouth into a bitter smile, unable to keep the derision from his tone. Hell, he didn't try. "Or marry Tyler Reinhold, and watch your father suffer the ruin of his reputation and the loss of his company, face federal charges and jail. Those are your options."

She tried to contain the small flinch but failed. Again that damned guilt reared its stubborn head, and again he squelched it. He couldn't afford sympathy or remorse. Not with his revenge so close he could taste the cold bite of it.

Could already feel the fifteen-year-old weight of the promise to his father lightening from his shoulders.

"Having a heart that's three sizes too small must be really convenient for business," she said. Surprise darted across her features, as if the sarcastic words had shocked her as much as him.

He barely managed to swallow his bark of laughter. He'd bet his left nut she hadn't meant to let the comment fly. Not the poised, flawlessly polite Sydney Blake. That he'd apparently ruffled her enough for that damn composure to slip sent a warm slide of pleasure through him.

"You'll turn my head with such flattery," he drawled. "Most people just claim I don't have a heart."

A muscle along her delicate jaw flexed, and he had the impression of her clenching her teeth and imprisoning a particularly impolite retort. Probably started with *fuck* and culminated in *you.* "How will you keep him from being charged? If you know about his"—her fingers curled into fists on her lap, the knuckles paling—"practices, then surely others do as well. How do I know after I marry you, he won't still end up in court?"

"As of now, his crimes haven't been discovered by the public or the SEC. I have certain sources within the Blake Corporation—"

"Spies," she snapped.

He shrugged. "—who have kept me informed. No one outside the company knows about the fraud your father has committed. Yet."

Greed. Power. Money. Those were Jason Blake's gods. Worshipping at their altars, he'd shattered Lucas's family, broken his father. Before Jason's betrayal, Robert Ellison had been a proud, commanding man, his only blind spot his selfish, spoiled, and unfaithful wife. Robert had expected backstabbing and perfidy from his business competition—not from his best friend.

She stared at him with something that resembled pity, a faint half smile curving her lips. "I hate to disappoint you, but if you think marrying me will hurt my father, you're sorely mistaken. Will he be angry over the embarrassment of me publicly abandoning Tyler? Yes. But ultimately, one wealthy, connected son-in-law will be just as fine as another."

He lowered his arms, frowning. Did she really believe that bullshit? A man as vain and image conscious as Jason handing his daughter over to a street fighter–turned–businessman? To men like her father, breeding and origins mattered as much as the income total on a profit and loss statement. And everyone knew Lucas Oliver was the adopted son of Duncan Oliver, a blue-collar construction worker from the South Side of Chicago.

"I think you underestimate your value, Sydney."

The smile widened and, for an instant, increased in sadness. "No, I'm not. You're overestimating."

What the hell did that mean? The question hovered on his tongue, but he swallowed the words. They—her response and the insane need to delve deeper into the unmistakable sorrow behind the enigmatic statement—didn't matter. Neither would keep him from carrying out his plan.

"What did he do to you?" she continued. "Back out of a deal? Cost you money?" Her lips twisted into a hard, cynical smile that somehow seemed blasphemous on her pretty mouth. "Sleep with your wife or girlfriend? It must've been something truly horrible for you to consider marriage to a woman you don't know a comparative cost."

"Oh, it's comparative," he murmured.

"In other words, it's none of my business. And if your revealing the truth behind your motives is part of my terms?"

"I've stated the terms, Sydney. They're nonnegotiable."

Her shoulders stiffened until he imagined one brisk wind might crack her in half. "What about fidelity?" she asked.

He stilled. The low question punched through his chest and exposed the dark, mottled place on his soul that contained the rage, hurt, and humiliation of overhearing his parents argue over his mother's serial adultery. Of witnessing her infidelity firsthand at his thirteenth birthday party, when she and a friend's father had sneaked off to fuck in the pool house.

He reached up to touch the scar over his eye, beat back the hot waves of anger and pain throbbing inside him. And studied the socialite sitting before him with her rigid frame and unreadable expression.

"Do you want it?" he asked.

"I demand it," she stated flatly. "If our intent is to convince everyone we're in love, then breaking the marriage vows before they're even dry will kind of taint the image."

"I don't think that pretense is necessary. I just need your hand in marriage, not your affection."

"I didn't offer it," she snapped. "And you're wrong. People will not easily accept this engagement. Especially since they're friends and associates with Tyler and his family. They don't know you, and after news of our relationship becomes public, you will be viewed, at best, as an interloper. Yes, they will do business with you, but most of those deals are initiated and discussed at social events. And those are ruled

over by the women—the wives and daughters of those busi-
nessmen. If they don't invite you or me because of our supposed betrayal of their own—Dad *and* Tyler—marriage to
me won't matter a damn. The only thing people will be more
likely to forgive is a story of a grand, passionate affair. After
all"—her lips curled into a hard, jaded smile that somehow
seemed alien on her—"everyone adores a love story with a
happily ever after."

Damn. She made perfect sense. Since his arrival in Boston, he'd been marginally welcomed into the insular circle of
Boston's elite and privileged. The social set was a tight-knit
group not easily infiltrated, and stealing Sydney from one of
the more influential members wouldn't sit well with them.
He couldn't afford to be ostracized. Not when business and
social lines ran side by side, often intersecting. And not when
a significant number of the accounts in Jason Blake's wealth
management firm hailed from the greater Boston area. After Lucas claimed ownership of the company—which he
would, once the financial part of his plan came together—
they would become his clients and stockholders.

Anger flared in his veins. At himself. He hadn't made it
this far by neglecting to weigh and analyze every variable in a
decision, personal and professional. Yet desire for revenge had
given him tunnel vision. How fucked up would it be to grasp
control of his enemy's corporation only to lose clients, reputation, and money to the fickle loyalties and morals of a few?

But even more…terrifying—screw it, yes, terrifying.
Even more terrifying was the fact that he'd placed himself in
the position to be humiliated like his father. Short of chaining
Sydney to his wrist, he could no more control her actions—
particularly what she decided to do with her vagina—than

his father could've controlled his mother's.

He'd yet to meet a woman who didn't scheme, lie, or cheat. He knew they existed, but his money seemed to bring out the worst in the ones who came near him.

"Fine," he drawled, arching an eyebrow. "I have no problem keeping my dick in my pants." He tilted his head to the side. "But from my experience, it's women who seem to have the issue keeping one out of theirs. We'll see if you prove different."

Her gasp blasted in the room seconds before she shoved her chair back and shot to her feet. She stalked forward, erasing the distance between them in two short, stiff strides. Outrage spiked color along her cheekbones. "Go. To. Hell."

Did it make him a depraved bastard that her fury hardened his cock? Slowly, he rose to his full height. Claimed the last remaining step that separated them. He lowered his head until he could detect the dark green flecks in her hazel eyes. Until the soft pants between her parted lips fluttered over his. Until he could taste the flavor of her kiss on her breath.

Until the need to consume that sweet scent and the owner of it roared through him like a freight train with faulty brakes. The unprecedented hunger should've had him shifting away from her, inserting much-needed space. Should've had him bolting away from the danger that had *led around by your dick* scrawled all over it.

Move. Run. Retreat. He should—

He slid a hand up her arm, over her shoulder, and cupped her nape. The warm, vulnerable skin seared his palm while the sleek, thick ponytail of dark hair caressed his fingers. He pressed his fingers into the side of her throat, the tips stroking the tendon running under the graceful column. She shivered.

Standing so close together, no way in hell he missed the tell-tale tremor. From where did it originate? Fear? No, not fear. Though she trembled against him, her glare condemned him to the same pit she'd ordered him to seconds earlier.

But there was something else mingling with the anger. He peered closer. Desire? Desire demanding he back her up against the wall, unwrap the dress held together by two simple ties, and unveil the body he'd been fantasizing about for two long, frustrating-as-hell nights?

Maybe. After all, there was a thin line between love and hate. Or in their case, lust and loathing.

"Been to hell, sweetheart," he whispered. "Have the T-shirt and refrigerator magnet to prove it." When her gaze flicked toward the scar, he smirked and added, "That, too." His fingers paused mid-stroke, his grip tightening. "If you betray me, I'll make your life miserable."

Long, feminine fingers skimmed up his arm…circled his neck. Squeezed. "Ditto."

For the first time in more years than he could remember, laughter—true, clean laughter—rolled in his gut, past his chest, and burst past his lips. Even to his own ears, the rumble of it sounded rusty, worse for wear. Few things surprised him, much less genuinely delighted him. Even fewer people challenged or braved the Beast. She'd done all three.

Again, that blast of warning ricocheted through him.

Caution. Evade. Leave. Don't—

He nipped her bottom lip. She stiffened, jerked away, but he'd anticipated the move and cupped the back of her head. When she didn't resist, he smoothed a palm up her throat with his other hand. Rubbed his thumb over one of those glorious, patrician cheekbones.

"One last item on the agenda, Sydney," he murmured. "You're demanding fidelity, and I'll give you that. But if I intended to be celibate, I would've become a priest."

Her lips twisted. "So you want conjugal visitation?"

He chuckled. "Cute." Swept another caress over her skin. "That's the second time you've intimated I'm taking away your choice. Does it make you feel better to believe I'm forcing you? Have you been giving in to people's wishes so long, believing I'm taking away your power is comfortable and safe for you? Sorry, you have choices. Even in marrying me. Even in coming to my bed. But, baby, let's not pretend you don't want to be there. That you haven't wondered what being under me…over me…would be like." Her breath hitched against his mouth, and he nodded, that small reaction as good as a resounding yes. "Yeah, you have," he growled, then surrendered to the need clawing at him since she'd walked into his office. Hell, since he'd heard her voice on the phone.

So he took. Conquered. Devoured.

A too-quiet voice of reason argued he should be gentler, tender, coax her into the kiss with soft brushes of lips over lips. But the moment his mouth touched hers—game over. With a low rumble, he swallowed the whimper she released, claiming her. Angling his head, he thrust his tongue between her parted lips, sweeping the sweet interior, thrusting, sucking, inviting her to tangle with him. Hesitantly, she met him, returning the sensual caress with cautious strokes that soon became bolder, hotter, wetter. Groaning, he pressed closer, demanded more. Every flutter and lick of her tongue against his traced and teased his cock. He lowered a hand to the curve of her hip, palmed it. Again, that image of his fingers gripping her flesh as he rode her, driving deep into a pussy he instinctively knew would be tight as a fist.

Damn it, he wanted more. He wanted to brand her with his mouth, touch, cock.

He wanted to drown in her heat. Become lost in it…

What the hell? He jerked his head up, abruptly ending the kiss. His chest rose and fell on the harsh breaths rushing from between his lips. Lost in her heat, in her. The dangerous thought rattled in his head as clear as a snake's furious warning. One kiss. One fucking kiss, and already he was slinging purple prose around like a damn poet. How many men—including his father—had allowed sex and lust to hoodwink them into believing in love? Silently, he snorted. Love. Thank God the much-lauded concept that made people lose their goddamn minds wasn't part of this bargain.

Revenge. Retribution. Justice. And yeah, sex. Blistering sex, if that kiss was any indication, but not emotion. Not *love*.

Stepping back, he inhaled…and wished he hadn't. Sensual, warm honeysuckle taunted him. Hell, was that her soap? Shampoo? Lotion? Part of him wanted to purge the scent from his senses. And the other half hungered to strip her naked, bare all that honey-and-cream skin, and stroke his body over hers, drench himself in her special perfume.

He took another step back.

Her thick fringe of lashes fluttered then lifted, revealing eyes clouded with passion. And he almost reclaimed that space. Damn. Pivoting on his heel, he rounded his desk, placing the furniture between them. And he still didn't trust himself. Not when she pressed her fingertips to her lips, damp from their kiss. Not when her gaze shifted to him, awe whispering through the desire.

Not when his zipper was doing an Etch A Sketch impression against his dick.

"I take it we have a deal," he said, his voice, hoarse with lust, rougher than he intended.

She blinked. Dropped her hand to her side. The sensual pleasure cleared from her expression as if it'd never softened her lovely features. Her frame stiffened, her shoulders straightening. He could almost perceive the wall of propriety slamming down between them. Too late. He'd glimpsed the carnal creature hidden behind the facade of decorum. This…arrangement might be in the name of vengeance, but their marriage wouldn't be in name only. He'd tasted her passion. And he craved more.

She stared at him. "You fight dirty, Lucas Oliver," she whispered.

"There's no other way to fight, Sydney," he mocked just as softly. "One week."

She blinked. "What? One week for what?"

"Before we're married."

Her head snapped back as if clipped by a verbal punch. "Are you kidding me? That's not enough time."

"This isn't going to be some huge event splashed over the papers. We don't need more time."

"I. Do," she gritted out. "Two weeks. At least."

He studied her, noted the glint in her eyes that hinted she was rapidly approaching the limits of her temper. God, that would be something to see. Sydney, letting go, uninhibited. Especially since a hint of what it would be like still tingled against his mouth.

"Fine," he conceded, not analyzing why he didn't push the issue. "Two weeks."

A tense silence, heavy with an invisible but palpable force, hummed in the room.

"How long?" she asked. "How long before I'm free?"

That shouldn't have stung. But fuck if it didn't. Hell, marriage was a trap designed to break spirits and trick people into losing their identities, voice, and pride all under the guise of surrender, trust, and the most deceptive of them all, love. But it was a trap he was willingly caging himself in. With her.

"One year," he ground out. That's all he needed for the plans he'd already set in motion to come to fruition. And by then, he'd almost certainly be gnawing at his foot to escape the ball and chain around it. "You'll leave with a healthy divorce settlement for your trouble."

"For my trouble? Do you define trouble as hurting my family, humiliating Tyler and his family, and ruining my reputation?" She snorted. "Keep your money. But I do want a contract drawn up." Ice and suspicion dripped from her tone. "I want a written, legal, binding contract that you will not send my father to jail and will leave him alone."

Leave Jason alone? Did she actually believe their engagement and marriage would be the end of it? Yes, both would cause Jason embarrassment and have him scrambling to make excuses to the Reinhold family. But by removing Tyler and his family's financial backing from the equation, Jason would be firmly trapped in the hole his greed had dug. And while Lucas did plan to return Blake Corporation to the black, the funds came with a price. For the past two years, Jason had been steadily releasing more and more stock to cover his fraudulence. And Lucas had been quietly purchasing each share as they became available through the different companies under Bay Bridge Industries' conglomerate umbrella. By the time he revealed his true identity to Jason Blake, it would be as a majority stockholder. And the other man would be reduced to nothing more than a figurehead of the company he'd ruined his best friend for. Lucas wasn't quite there yet. But he would be—soon.

Part of him longed to spill the truth to Sydney about her father, to rip the mask away and expose the ugly, rancid reality of the man she championed. The man she was willing to literally sign her life over for. But he'd come too far. It'd been too long. And he couldn't risk her revealing his plans to Jason. Not now.

So close. His breath rattled in his chest. *God, I'm so close.*

And a woman—no matter how much he craved her taste or wanted to be buried balls deep inside her—was worth his revenge. His father's retribution.

He smiled, and its arctic temperature matched hers. "Of course," he drawled. "I require written, binding documents with all my transactions."

For a moment, her eyes closed, and though she tried, she wasn't quick enough to conceal her flinch as his verbal blow struck. He clenched his jaw. Hell, yeah, he was a cold, grade-A bastard, but damn it, she hadn't deserved that barb.

Frustrated, he balled his fingers into a tight fist. "I—"

"You really are the beast they call you," she murmured, then turned, and spine straight, head high, strode from his office. The quiet click of the door closing as effective as if she'd slammed it.

So the kitten had claws. And her scratch had drawn blood.

Best he not forget that.

Chapter Seven

For the second time in as many days, Sydney stood outside her father's corporate office building. Yesterday, anxiety and a sliver of hope had filled her chest. Today, that hope had been obliterated with Terry's confession and her signature on a legal, binding contract.

By the time she'd returned home from Lucas's office, the contract detailing the terms of their agreement had arrived in her in-box. Almost as if he'd already had the document drawn up in anticipation of her acquiescence to his blackmail. She scoffed. No "almost" about it—Lucas Oliver was one of the most arrogant men she'd ever encountered. He'd probably harbored no doubt she would ultimately surrender.

With the document printed out, perused, signed, and mailed back to him by that afternoon, she could find no reason to put off revealing the news of her broken engagement to her father. Dread curdled in her stomach. She swallowed hard, forcing down the nausea born of fear and worry. While a fighter used his fists to pummel and inflict pain, her father employed words and subzero silences to bruise and maim. She'd been on the receiving end of those debilitating blows of disapproval too many times to keep an accurate tally. Yet every instance seemed like the first, the most hurtful.

And now she had to face her father and reveal she was not only going to humiliate him by publicly ending her relationship with Tyler, but possibly ruin a long business and personal relationship with the Reinholds.

He wouldn't know that in dealing this blow, she would also be saving the very thing he loved most. She'd failed him once—she wouldn't do so again.

She sucked in a breath, already bracing herself against the cutting condemnation and scorn.

"Sydney."

Startled, she jerked her head up, heart in her throat.

She blinked. Stared. Blinked again.

Lucas stood next to her, the brisk October breeze trailing through his dark hair as if it, too, couldn't resist the lure of the thick strands.

She knew the feeling. Damn it.

To be so…"attracted" was such an anemic description of the almost visceral response she experienced at the sight of his tall, lean, powerful frame, his stunning, scarred face and incisive turquoise eyes. One summer while vacationing at Martha's Vineyard, several of the local teens had set off firecrackers on the stretch of beach in back of her family's home. Even now, years later, she could hear the sizzle, spark, and pop before the explosion of sound and heat. That build-up and blast perfectly captured her body's reaction to Lucas, as evidenced yesterday by that foreplay innocuously called a kiss. Desire had sunk its greedy talons into her, and she'd surrendered with an embarrassingly minimal fight. In that instant when he'd cupped her head, controlling and limiting her movement as he thrust his tongue between her lips and destroyed every preconceived notion of passion she'd possessed, she been hit with an image of what sex with him would be like. Scorching. Demanding. Wild. A touch dirty…

Two weeks.

Jesus, in two weeks she would be married to him. Be in his bed. Firecrackers erupted into a full-scale explosive assault. Fear, anxiety, and that traitorous heat mushroomed until she fairly vibrated with them.

Wait. What am I doing? Guilt wormed through the desire, coating the heat in oil. This man had planned and sought to devastate her father and was using her to do it. How could she want him, feel anything for him but loathing?

She was even more of a traitor.

"What are you doing here?" she snapped, her inner turmoil sharpening her tone to a razor's edge. When she'd called him yesterday to let him know she'd mailed the contract back, he'd asked about her plans of telling her father about the broken engagement. She hadn't expected him to show up this morning. No doubt to gloat over the carnage.

"You're here," he said flatly.

The two simple words ignited a chain reaction of flutters in her belly, but as quickly as those butterflies burst open, she forced them back into their cocoons. From a different man, his statement might have meant he cared. But she was just a pawn in Lucas's plan; he'd placed her in the predicament of having to crush her father's hopes. Not that she desired his affection. This arrangement had nothing to do with love and respect, and as long as she remembered who she was dealing with, her heart would remain uninvolved. She couldn't be hurt.

"Translation, you couldn't resist witnessing my father's reaction to our engagement for yourself." She returned her gaze to the intimidating, imposing tower of steel and glass. A perfect reflection of her father. "Or you don't trust me to go in there by myself. Are you afraid I'll give him hand signals, tipping him off that this whole thing is a horrible farce?"

"Sydney."

"What?"

"You're stalling. Why?" He shifted closer, his large hand settling at the base of her spine. Heat from his touch infiltrated the layers of her light coat and dress, setting the nerves there to dancing. She sidestepped, attempting to place more space between them and dislodge his hand, but he followed. The hard plane of his chest nudged her shoulder, and two long fingers gripped her chin in an unyielding grip, tipping her face up. "Are you afraid? Has your father ever hurt you?" The question ended on a low growl, his eyebrows forming a dark, forbidding vee.

Not in the way you're implying. "No, of course not. He's never laid a hand on me." She jerked her head, but his hold didn't slacken, and she glared at him. "Do you mind?"

His eyes narrowed, but to her relief, he dropped his hold and withdrew several inches, so every breath she inhaled didn't contain the scent of fresh spring rain.

"After you." He ducked his head in a mock bow and swept his arm in the direction of the entrance, a small, sardonic smile curving his mouth.

She didn't bother with a reply, all her focus on the glass

door that seemed to loom and expand like the gaping, sharp-toothed maw of a predator the longer she stared at it. *Go and get this over with. Yes, he's going to be angry—furious, even—but it's for him. All of this is for him.*

The mantra scrolled through her mind like a newsreel as she entered the office building, boarded the elevator, and emerged on the same floor she'd visited the day before—the day her world had transformed from a staid but stable existence to a precarious minefield full of lies, pitfalls, and explosive secrets.

"Good morning," Sydney greeted the receptionist stationed outside her father's inner sanctum. The lovely brunette returned her smile with a cool, professional version. *Hmm.* Sydney studied the twenty-something who couldn't have been much older than her. *She's new.* Had her father slept with this one yet? Well, if they were lovers, she hoped the woman didn't embrace illusions that Jason would leave his wife for her like the last assistant had. That one had arrived at the house and had been firmly set straight by Charlene. Her father might screw around on his wife, but he wasn't willing to risk social suicide by divorcing her for a younger model—not when Charlene and her family name carried as much weight in Boston society as Jason's.

But it could be her cynicism was premature. Maybe her father had left this one alone...

"Good morning. Do you have an appointment with Jason—I mean, Mr. Blake?" The woman didn't bat an eyelash at her blunder, but she did confirm Sydney's suspicion. Sydney glanced at Lucas. He shared the same magnetism, charm, and power her father wielded. Two men cut from the same expensive, beautiful cloth. And this new plaything of her father's served as a 3-D reminder of why falling for a man as gorgeous, powerful, and ruthless as Lucas Oliver would be the height of insanity.

"No, we don't have an appointment. But could you let him know his daughter is here?"

Surprise flared in the woman's gaze seconds before she picked up the phone. "Mr. Blake, your daughter is here to see you." Pause. "Yes, sir. I will." Hanging up the receiver, she rose. "If you'll follow me."

Aware of Lucas's quiet but commanding presence close behind her, Sydney trailed behind the assistant, taking note of the minute changes to the decor since her last visit a few years earlier. Though the Blake Corporation had been in her family for three generations, Sydney had only dropped by her father's office a handful of times. He hadn't been the kind of dad who bounced his children on his lap, teaching them the ropes of the business they would one day inherit. Maybe if Jay had lived, he might've been that kind of father. But...

She entered the office with a murmur of thanks to the receptionist. Jason didn't glance up from the work on his desk as the door shut with a soft but ominous click. "Sydney, this is an inconvenient time to show up unannounced," he admonished, his tone clipped. As usual, his barely concealed impatience toward her grated, but even more so with Lucas there to witness it. "I have a meeting shortly, so make this fast. What—" He glanced up, the irritation in his tight-lipped expression giving way to shock as his scrutiny swept past her and landed on Lucas. Color slashed across his mahogany cheekbones as he slowly stood. "Lucas Oliver." He rounded his desk, arm outstretched. "My assistant didn't mention you were here."

Sydney absorbed the dismissive blow without flinching; she was used to coming in second—or third or fourth—behind business. But beside her, Lucas stiffened. She glanced up at him. But his shadowed contemplation and relaxed mouth didn't betray the tension pulling him as tight as a strung bow. His low, cool tone as he shook her father's hand didn't relay the contempt that would drive a man to blackmail a woman for revenge.

Better keep that forefront in her mind.

Lucas Oliver was a consummate actor. And his reaction hadn't been out of offense on her behalf. No, standing in this office, he hovered on the cusp of his plans coming to fruition. That kind of anticipation would cause the tautness in his large frame.

Vengeance, not concern.

"Excuse me if I seem rude, but did we have an appointment today?" her father asked, a tiny furrow crinkling his brow.

"No, we didn't." Lucas pressed a hand to her spine, and she fought the instinctive urge to shift away. To move away from the deceit in the protective gesture. "Sydney and I are together. I apologize for the unexpected intrusion, but we need to speak with you."

Jason's gaze swung from Lucas to her. Confusion and a deepening suspicion darkened his eyes. "Is that so?" he murmured.

Fear snaked up her chest and circled her throat. It turned her mouth into an arid landscape, and the words became mired on her tongue.

"Sydney." Her father stepped forward, and at the same

time, Lucas edged closer, his lean hip pressing against hers. Jason paused, his gaze intercepting the small movement. Surprise erased the burgeoning anger, but only for a moment. "Sydney," he repeated, the soft note a warning. "What is going on here?"

She forced a calmness into her voice that belied the chaotic storm twisting in her head like a late summer storm. "Dad, Lucas has asked me to marry him. And I—" She paused, the pounding of her heart momentarily halting her breath. Then the hand on her back moved, smoothed down her arm. His big palm pressed against hers, his fingers tangled with hers. A show of support? Or a feigned act of affection for her father's sake? At this moment, she didn't care. She curled her fingers, holding tight. "And I accepted his proposal," she continued.

Jason's eyes widened, his lips slackened, shock bleeding the color from his complexion, leaving a waxy pallor behind. Alarmed, she loosed Lucas's grip and moved forward, arm outstretched. Jesus, what had she done? "Dad…"

His palm slammed up, halting her mid-step as if an invisible wall had sprung up between them. Slowly, his astonishment faded. Crimson bloomed under his skin, mottling his smooth brown skin. A white line outlined the thin, hard line of his mouth like the garish, smudged lipstick of a faded beauty queen.

"Tell me this is a joke, Sydney," he snapped. "Or a pathetic bid for attention."

She flinched as his words slapped at her. A bid for attention. As if she were five instead of twenty-five. Inhaling a deep breath, she tucked the throbbing pain and resentment in a pocket of her heart. The same pocket where she'd hidden the hurt, bitterness, and guilt from similar remarks over the years. The compartment was close to bursting at the seams.

"It's not a joke, Dad," she murmured. "I'm sorry."

"Sorry?" he bit out. "Sorry? Do you have any idea what you're doing? What you're doing to me, to your mother? Think what this will do to our reputation. You can't just toss aside Tyler Reinhold. You were lucky he showed interest in you in the first place, much less proposed marriage."

A brilliant starburst of pain exploded in her chest. She stared at her father, his rage beating against her skin like crashing waves of heat. Inside herself, she curled into a fetal position, blocking her vulnerable organs from another emotional kick. On the outside, though, she squared her shoulders, notched her chin up. Bracing herself for the next punch of his anger, for his verbal jabs.

"I disagree." The cold, hard objection came a second before an unyielding wall of muscle supported her shoulders and spine. Firm hands bracketed her hips, holding her steady. "Reinhold was fortunate. He had Sydney—beautiful, intelligent, kind, loyal Sydney. Your daughter. And when she decided to share her life with him, he should've been down on his knees thanking her and God, because in that moment he became the luckiest man on earth. Just like I felt when she agreed to be mine."

Beautiful, intelligent, kind, loyal. Lies, lies, lies, her reason blared like a foghorn on a dark, overcast night. All for the benefit of the ruse. But her heart—her heart that had been nicked and bruised by neglect, low self-esteem, and guilt—soaked up his words, gorged on them like a person feasting after a long trek through an arid, barren wasteland.

"You've known her for five minutes, and you assume to

tell me who my daughter is?"

"Yes," Lucas stated, voice flat, definite. "Because it's obvious if you can make a comment denigrating her worth, her value, then you don't know her at all."

Jason winced—or maybe it was her imagination. A hallucination caused by her desperation to find acceptance in her father's grim, forbidding expression. "If you believe you'll get your hands on my wealth and connections through my daughter, you're sorely mistaken. I'll cut her off, disown her if she goes through with this"—he waved a hand back and forth between her and Lucas—"this farce."

"I don't need your money," Lucas replied. "And neither will Sydney. But she does need you and your wife."

Jason's gaze cut to her, and the derision and disappointment there scored her. She hadn't glimpsed such animosity and helplessness since...since Jay.

"Daddy," she whispered, her throat tightening around the last syllable. It had been years since she'd called him that. Years since he'd been her laughing, loving daddy instead of distant, cold Dad. Only desperation had squeezed the more intimate name from her lips. *I'm doing this for him. I'm saving his business, guaranteeing his freedom. Even if he can't stand the sight of me after this.* "I know this sounds crazy and irresponsible to you. And Lucas is right. I don't want to lose you or Mom." She spread her hands wide, palms up as if they contained the answers she couldn't supply him. "But I don't love Tyler, and spending the rest of my life in a loveless marriage would ultimately make both of us miserable. He deserves to be with a woman who can give him all of herself. He deserves to be happy. If I went through with the marriage, neither one of us would be."

Truth rang in her words and resonated in her spirit. Just a few days ago, she'd been content with the life set before her. Passionless but stable. Predictable but dependable. Loveless but respectful. While she'd been ready to consign herself to that life, had Tyler? Or one day, would he wake up and realize she wasn't enough? She wasn't pretty enough, witty enough, accomplished enough. And would that be the day he sought out other women? Like her father had. And would that also be the day she became the reflection of her mother? An exquisitely coiffed, composed mannequin on the outside while seething with humiliation, hurt, and rejection on the inside? Filling the emotional holes in her life with committees, fund-raising, and parties? Sydney had agreed to marry Tyler to avoid her parents' fate…and had started the gilded road to that exact destination.

Not that she would find peace or a happily ever after with Lucas. But after their year together lapsed, she would be free—free of the strangling noose of family obligations, societal expectations, social condemnation, and guilt. The awful albatross of guilt.

Even without her father's support or the financial set-tlement Lucas had offered her, she would survive. She pos-sessed money of her own, thanks to the inheritance from her maternal grandmother three years earlier. She could live her life the way she desired. The way she dreamed. She could return to school for a degree in education. Spend more time at the youth center. Discover who Sydney Blake truly was.

And love her.

For a second—a blip in time—her father's expression softened. But the seed of hope didn't take root before his eyes and mouth hardened. Maybe it'd been her need for his love and approval that had her imagining the compassion she'd glimpsed. Ecstasy had nothing on desperation when it came to creating hallucinations.

"Have you told Tyler yet?" her father demanded.

"No. I wanted to speak with you first."

"Good." Jason nodded sharply. "Then we can forget this foolishness, and Tyler won't have to know about any of it." He clapped his hands together and turned away as if his proclamation settled the matter. And she couldn't blame him. In the past, his final word would've been just that—the final word. She would've caved and obeyed like the perfect, dutiful daughter.

But not this time. She couldn't. His freedom depended on her disappointing him.

"I'm sorry, Dad." Her apology halted him mid-turn. Slowly, like a wind-up toy, he pivoted, facing her again. Grief and regret swamped her, dragging her under its suffocating tide. "I can't," she rasped.

His eyebrows arched high, surprise flaring in his eyes before they narrowed. "Sydney, if you go through with this engagement and marriage, you're choosing him"—he jerked his chin toward Lucas, who stood quietly behind her—"over your family. Think very carefully about your next words to me."

Part of her wanted to scream like a banshee on a battlefield. *I already chose you.* The cry ricocheted against the walls of her mind. Instead she remained silent.

"So you've made your decision," Jason said, his voice a harsh whip across her heart. "Where should I have your belongings delivered?"

"Dad, I—"

"No. You aren't welcome in the home I've provided for twenty-five years. We have nothing more to say to each other if your next words aren't you've changed your mind about going through with this silliness and will honor your commitment with Tyler. Loyalty, Sydney. I believed I'd taught you family loyalty, but it appears you learned nothing. When you come to your senses and realize we are more important than a man you've just met and know nothing about, then you can return home. Until then, all I want to hear from you is an address."

She sucked in a breath, blinking to beat back the tiny pinpricks of tears. *Tell him*, a small, insidious voice whispered in her head. *Just tell him the whole truth, and he'll forgive you.* Her lips parted, the confession almost spilling from her tongue. But an image flashed across her mind's eye. Her father, disgraced as he faced a judge and jury. Her father, handcuffs shackling his wrists as he was led away from her mother, from Sydney. Her father, old, worn, broken, speaking to her from behind a panel of Plexiglas.

Jason crossed his arms. "Sydney. An address."

An address. An address. *God, I don't know.* She was adrift, a lone leaf floating on a biting, brisk autumn breeze. Out of all the scenarios she'd envisioned, being thrown out of her home hadn't been one. Where would she go? She had friends, but none close enough to ask if they would take her in. Or more importantly, none close enough to not gossip about her circumstances…

"She's staying with me." Lucas squeezed her hip as if warning her not to disagree. As if she could. Objecting would require working lungs and a tongue. "I'll leave my address with your assistant." Shifting to the side, he tangled his fingers with hers once more. "And she didn't choose me over her family or transfer her loyalty from you to me. On the contrary, you chose your pride over her happiness and well-being. If you change your mind about abandoning your daughter, you know where to find her."

Not allowing her a chance to speak or Jason an opportunity to reply, he turned and led her from her father's office. Numb, she remained silent, frozen as he shut the door behind them.

"Are you all right?" he asked once they were safely down the hall.

The question seemed to reach her through layers and layers of wool, distant and muffled. God, no, she wasn't okay. Everything she'd known—her parents, her home, her identity—had been blown to hell and back in a matter of minutes. As flawed as her family and life were, they'd belonged to her. They were familiar. In their own dysfunctional way, they were her safety net...her norm. And now what did she have? No home. No family. Friends who bent and wavered in the direction of the ever-changing societal wind. A man who detested her father so much he had no qualms about stripping her of her will and power to obtain his revenge.

No. "All right" had caught the last red-eye flight out of Boston, and "crazy as shit" had just stepped into the building.

"I don't know where your father's assistant went, but she'll probably return soon." The dark gray of his shirt and darker silver of his tie filled her vision as his spring-rain scent wrapped her in its embrace. "For the next couple of minutes, don't think about who's watching or about appearing weak. Instead, for these two minutes, lean on me. We won't talk about it, won't ever bring it up. And I promise not to use it against you." He cupped her nape gently but firmly, tugged her closer and into the strong, hard lines of his body. "It'll be our secret," he murmured against her hair.

The low, dark velvet of his voice lured her in as much as his tender, insistent grip. *For just a moment.* She rested her forehead on the wide plane of his shoulder. Allowed her lashes to drift shut. She was so tired. The weight of her father's displeasure and rejection settled across her shoulders like a dumbbell she had no hope of bench-pressing. Instead it pressed down on her, squeezing the air from her lungs, constricting her chest, weakening her legs. Yes, for just a moment, she'd borrow his strength, lean on him…

"Sydney?"

She stiffened. *Oh. Damn.*

Slowly, she straightened, turned. And faced Tyler.

His gaze switched from her to Lucas and back to her, a frown drawing down his dark brown eyebrows.

"Sydney," he said, stepping closer, his arm outstretched. "What's going on? Is something wrong?"

Regret for the humiliation and hurt she was about to inflict clenched her belly. She harbored no doubt that Tyler cared for her, yes, but the affection a man should possess for his wife? No. But he would still suffer from the public rejection. He would still be whispered and gossiped about. And she would lose a friend.

"Tyler," she pleaded. With a quick glance toward the empty conference room on their right, she shifted to the side, neatly avoiding his hand. Knowing in a few moments he wouldn't want anything to do with her, much less invite her touch. "Can we talk?"

Tyler hesitated, then nodded. As she moved to follow

him, Lucas aligned himself beside her. Once again refusing to let her face the backlash alone.

How ironic.

Suddenly alone of family and friends, her one ally was the Beast of Bay Bridge.

• • •

Sydney stared up at Lucas's Back Bay brownstone. The structure resembled its owner: elegant, striking, imposing. And was now her only sanctuary.

No, not sanctuary. Because that implied while she might be safe — physically — and off the street, it also suggested she felt comfortable, warm, sheltered, peaceful. Those couldn't be further from the truth.

Behind her, Lucas's driver removed her suitcases from the trunk of the limo, lining them along the curb. Apparently, before she and Lucas could make it out of the building, her father had called and told her mother and housekeeper to pack up Sydney's belongings and have them delivered. Her and Lucas's arrival at her parents' home had expedited the delivery part of the command. That simply, that easily, her father had ushered her out of her home, his life. And now she stood on a sidewalk with her luggage, dependent on the mercy of a man who had none.

Not true, her conscience whispered. *Lucas immediately stepped in, defended you, offered you a place to stay.*

And he's also the person responsible for placing me in this situation, she countered.

God, she must be more exhausted than she believed to be debating points back and forth with herself.

Sighing, she hiked her tote higher on her shoulder. Personal and sentimental items the housekeeper had neglected to pack filled the tote. Pictures—of her parents, of Jay that she'd hidden away at the top of her closet. Books, journals, and pieces of jewelry from her grandmother.

"Come on inside," Lucas murmured, guiding her up the stone steps. Moments later, he opened the front door, and she stepped into the foyer. "I know you're tired. Let me give you a quick tour and then you can rest."

Nodding, she took her first inspection of his home.

She hadn't known what to expect—decor that shouted the wealth of its owner in every painting, piece of furniture, and decorative piece? Or an austere, minimalistic design straight out of the Spartans 'R' Us catalog? Reality fell somewhere in between.

Clean, uncluttered elegance, yet luxurious. Gorgeous landscapes adorned the walls, beautiful earth-toned furniture enhanced the gleaming cherrywood of the floors, banister, railings, and stairs. Airy rooms with high ceilings, large bay windows, and cavernous fireplaces welcomed people to come sit and visit. The entire brownstone belonged to him. The garden level contained his study, while the parlor level, where they'd entered, held the great room, another smaller living area, a bathroom, and an amazing kitchen. The top level had been renovated so the master bedroom occupied most of the space. Huge floor-to-ceiling windows dominated one wall, and late afternoon light poured into the room. Sumptuous, decadent. And perfect for the man standing next to her. She could easily imagine him lying on the almost sinfully large bed with its soaring four posters, the rich black bedspread pooling around his narrow waist, leaving his chest bare.

She reined in her too-vivid imagination and averted her too-enraptured regard.

"Your room is down the hall," he said, leaving the door to his bedroom open. As if in invitation.

Seconds later he opened the door to a smaller but no less exquisitely appointed bedroom. Her suitcases had beaten her there. *So this is where I'll live for the next year.*

As soon as the words ghosted through her head, a wave of exhaustion and loneliness broke over her, almost buckling her knees. Maybe she wavered or swayed, because from one breath to the next, Lucas's arms were surrounding her, holding her steady.

That fast, the surge of lethargy evaporated, leaving an electrical awareness popping and sizzling under her skin. She shuddered, detesting her visceral reaction. Why, of all people, did her heart pound and her body swell and pulse for this man? Even Tyler made more sense...

Oh, Jesus, Tyler.

Images of their confrontation bombarded her.

She'd prevented Lucas from accompanying her into the empty office while she broke the news to Tyler. Having Lucas there as a witness when she informed her fiancé—*former* fiancé—that their engagement was off had seemed unnecessarily cruel. And ultimately, she'd made the right call. God, Tyler's shock, disbelief. His rage.

"Are you seriously doing this to me, Sydney? I've always cared for you, respected you, and this is how you treat me? With betrayal and humiliation? What kind of person does that to someone she's supposed to love?"

She'd never proclaimed to love Tyler, had never even

spoken those words to him, but it hadn't lessened the hurt, the injustice of inflicting harm on a man who'd done nothing to deserve it. An apology had seemed pointless, but she'd given it to him anyway, along with his ring. But when he'd demanded an explanation, she couldn't give him the truth. And when he'd stalked away from her, hating her, she'd let him.

"Hey." Lucas gently turned her around, and on reflex, she clasped the waist she'd been fantasizing about only moments ago. As if singed, she dropped her hands to her sides. "Are you okay?"

She released a short bark of laughter. "Am I okay? I don't even know what that means anymore. In the space of a day, I've become public enemy number one, and I've been kicked out of my home. I'd say okay is a stretch."

A beat of silence passed between them.

"My offer from earlier still stands, Sydney," Lucas murmured. His big, elegant hand cradled her jaw, the pad of his thumb brushing over her cheekbone. His heavy-lidded perusal roamed her face, settling for an unnerving—tantalizing—amount of time on her trembling mouth. "Our secret," he rumbled, flattening a hand on the wall beside her head. The wall behind her, his tall, strong, wide-shouldered body in front of her. She should've felt threatened, at least indignant, but only traitorous molasses-thick warmth wound through her veins, heating her from the inside out, making her body suddenly feel three times heavier. "Let me hold you, touch you. Help you to forget this day even for a short time."

God. If he'd extended an apple to her along with his low, sensual words, he couldn't have been more of a temptation. And like Eve, she longed to take him up on his proposal, bite into and savor the delicious sweetness of it. She didn't doubt he could erase the last few hours from her mind with a pleasure that would leave her a quivering mess. He'd gift her with possibly hours of ecstasy-filled oblivion. Because his hooded, carnal gaze offered more than a simple hug or comforting words. And damn, if she didn't want it. Wanted him to sink into her with his powerful body, have her crying out for a different reason than grief and loneliness.

And then what?

Sex was part of their agreement, and when he'd initially mentioned it, she hadn't objected. No, he hadn't included it in the contract, as he'd implied, and in spite of the merciless-ness he was capable of, she didn't believe he would force her. But if she gave in to him now, the sex wouldn't be about blackmail, her father, or vengeance. It would be about what she wanted. Him. His hands on her body. Him filling her, pleasuring her.

When the sweat dried and the pleasure ebbed away, where would she be? No family, no fiancé, no pride, and vul-nerable, totally at his mercy. Yes, she'd surrendered to his blackmail, was now living in his home, but at this point he didn't control *her*. Not her will, her mind, her spirit.

But she suspected once she submitted to the stubborn and relentless hunger that blazed within her like a beach bonfire, she would forfeit the last of her power. Because a man like Lucas didn't leave women unscathed—didn't leave them whole.

A year from now, she had to emerge from this pact as *her*. She had to walk away strong. Not needy, broken, and craving a man who only wanted her for revenge's sake.

"As *kind* as your offer is," she said, pouring a wealth of

disdain into "kind," so there was no way he could misinterpret what she really believed about his suggestion, "I'm going to pass. You have a way of just glossing over the glaring fact that if not for the events you set in motion, I wouldn't be here in your house, estranged from my family, and my life tossed into a set of luggage. So forgive me if I decide not to lean on you."

Lucas studied her for a long moment, the emotion in his incisive scrutiny indiscernible. Finally, he pushed off the wall and straightened, his hand falling away from her.

And damn her body or the pathetic neediness — or both — that yearned to grasp his hand and return it to her face.

"If you change your mind, my bedroom is down the hall."

Before she could assure him that he shouldn't wait for the knock on the door, he strode away. Leaving her alone, aching, frustrated. And afraid.

Because she'd won this battle, but she couldn't shake the inescapable sense that he would win this war.

Chapter Eight

"What the hell?" Lucas exited the rear of the Mercedes Rolls-Royce limousine and stared at the three-story brick building. He shot a glance at James, his driver. "You're sure this is the correct address?"

James nodded. "Yes, sir."

Lucas returned his gaze to the building that dominated a small portion of the Washington Street block in the Oak Square area of Brighton. Its weathered brick, glass, and white shutters contrasted with the more modern appearance of the neighboring pizzeria and grocery store, making it appear older yet...refined. Maya Angelou Girls' Youth Center. The black sign with heavy gold lettering further lent a dignified, if worn, air. Like a dowager with her proud head still held high, demanding respect.

So what the hell was his fiancée and roommate of a week doing at a Brighton community center?

"Be right back," he informed his driver before striding

up the sidewalk and cement steps. As soon as he pulled open the wide front door, the scents of lemon wax and glue, with a whiff of chlorine, struck him, propelling him back to the many afternoons and evenings he'd spent at his Chicago neighborhood's youth center. When he'd first arrived in the unfamiliar city, thrust into a new family that consisted of an uncle—his father's half brother—whom he'd never met, the center with its huge basketball court, indoor track, and pool had been a godsend…and his sanity. And not just because of the various activities that permitted him to pound out his grief and anger. The quiet but stalwart presence of Michael, the teen youth counselor there, had granted him space and peace in the middle of the emotional squall Lucas had been cast into. Michael had been his first real friend in Chicago, even before Aiden. To this day, they remained in touch, going out for lunch and playing pickup games of basketball when Lucas returned home. Shit, where would he be now without Michael, who'd gifted him with an outlet for his rage and sorrow?

Jail. Or worse.

Lucas grimaced. Damn. Where had those thoughts come from? He refocused his attention on the long corridor he stood in rather than those initial dark weeks fifteen years ago. Continuing down the hall, he noticed the various artwork displayed on the walls. Drawings and paintings of landscapes—some of them quite beautiful—and projects on famous female Bostonians such as Abigail Adams, Bette Davis, Susan B. Anthony, and… He cocked his head to the side, grinned. Faith from *Buffy*? Apparently he wasn't the only fan of her badass character.

"Can I help you?"

Lucas turned away from his study of first ladies, actresses, suffragists, and vampire hunters to meet the direct gaze of a short, middle-aged woman. He quelled the instinctive urge to stutter an explanation, but just barely. Damn if she didn't remind him of his high school English teacher. That woman had been plain scary with her stern manner and steely gaze. This woman might have brown eyes instead of gray, unlined caramel skin instead of Ms. Gregory's pale, papery complexion, but they shared the same formidable air.

"Yes," he said. "I'm looking for Sydney Blake. She asked me to meet her here." He offered his hand. "I'm Lucas Oliver."

The woman arched an eyebrow. "Oh." She accepted his hand, gave it a brisk pump, then released it. "Sydney told us to expect you." Pivoting sharply on the heel of her low-heeled black pumps, she dipped her chin. "Follow me."

Left with little choice — and frankly, afraid not to obey — Lucas fell into step behind her, bemused. Clearly, she recognized his name, but to say she wasn't impressed was like saying King Kong was a simple gorilla who liked heights. A pretty huge understatement.

Moments later, she stopped in front of a closed door. Voices filtered past the thick wood and reached them in the hallway. Without glancing back at him, she cracked the door open and paused in the entrance. She didn't enter, and not relishing angering the dragon at the gate, he waited with her.

But then he caught a familiar voice and promptly forgot about her. Forgot the frosty welcome. Forgot everything but the husky, sin-and-satin tone that would've made a phone sex operator a shitload of money.

Sydney.

"So if the rule regarding the sentinels touching was false, what do you think was the Misgiver's purpose behind instilling this belief system?" Sydney glanced around the circle of about twenty teen girls surrounding her. Several of the girls bowed their heads over the ereaders they each held, while a few others peeked around, maybe trying to see who would answer first.

Finally, a young girl with an alarming array of different colors in her hair spoke up. "Division. So they would remain suspicious and afraid of one another and never share knowledge or information about themselves."

Sydney beamed. "Very good, Anna. Anyone else?"

"To keep them weak," a more timid voice added.

He zeroed in on the speaker, and noted the thin, small girl at the top of the circle, and the farthest away from Sydney. From her wide eyes and rapidly swaying legs, she seemed terrified to be the center of attention. "With no knowledge or unity, they were weaker and easier to control through fear and the unknown."

Sydney nodded, her grin for this girl not as wide, but softer, as if she understood the courage speaking out had cost the teen. As if she was proud of her and the effort. "Exactly," Sydney said. "Awesome insight, Lily."

The discussion continued, neither Sydney nor the girls noticing him and the woman hovering in the doorway, eavesdropping on what seemed to be a book club.

He didn't—couldn't—remove his gaze from Sydney. He hadn't seen her in three days. It'd been a week since they'd met with her father and Tyler. A week since she'd moved into his Back Bay brownstone, infusing the very atmosphere with her presence. Though she'd tried to avoid him—and for the most part succeeded—he felt her there. Caught the trace of her special scent as soon as he arrived home in the evenings. Caught the drum of water when she showered... and imagined all that golden skin slick and glistening. It was pure damn torture sleeping in the same house as her and not being able to trail his fingers down the erect line of her spine, the indent of her waist and flare of her hips. Not being allowed to bare and cup the beautiful curves of her breasts. Not permitted to fuck the sweet, hot flesh between her legs, feel her squeeze his cock like a tight fist. Or a wet, hungry mouth.

He ground his teeth together, his dick pulsing behind his zipper as if demanding, *what the hell?*

Which explained why he'd called her that morning and let her know he'd received an invitation for a charity fund-raising gala, and he'd accepted. He couldn't stand one more evening in the house with her, tempted by the suggestion of her. This party tonight would serve as their first appearance as an engaged couple. And he could touch her under the guise of head-over-ass in love while public scrutiny would ensure his behavior. Because right now, the prospect of being able to press his hand to the shallow dip above her perfect ass or nuzzle the fragrant, shadowed spot behind her ear... He would need more than his much-lauded control to keep himself in line.

But when James had pulled up outside the building, he hadn't been expecting...this. While growing up in Chicago, he'd been the recipient of attention lavished by idealistic, overeager case workers and photo-hungry socialites looking to be the next Great White Hope for underprivileged children. He could spot them at a hundred paces and either scare or piss them off at fifty. But that wasn't what he wit-nessed here.

Patience, affection, and delight lit her smile, impassioned her voice. Even the most jaded street kid could discern her true joy in being with these kids. Including him.

Something ancient and primal kicked hard inside him. His survival instinct. The intuition had never steered him wrong. And right now his instincts screamed at him to turn around, run—don't walk—to the nearest exit, and get the hell away from Sydney Blake. That she was a wild card. That she wasn't who she appeared to be. He couldn't trust some-one he couldn't read, someone whose motive he couldn't pinpoint. Ironic, considering everything people knew about him was a cleverly constructed cover. But this close to suc-cess, he couldn't afford an unknown. Especially when that unknown played such a vital part in his victory. The smart move would be to retreat, regroup, and reorganize. Without Sydney. Just walk away…

He remained in the doorway.

"So, we'll continue on Monday." She smiled, closed the cover of her ereader, and glanced up. And froze. The tender-ness in her hazel gaze faded, and the curves of her sensual, soft mouth hardened. That quickly the polite, aloof socialite appeared. A part of him damned her presence. Demanded the return of the vulnerable, approachable woman who'd talked, laughed, and listened to the teen girls who hung on every word she uttered as if they were tales of glittering vampires and shirtless werewolves.

Suddenly, he found himself the focus of twenty-one pairs of eyes. One shuttered, the others curious. Hell, standing in front of a table full of investors and stockholders had never made him this uncomfortable.

"Sydney, you have a visitor," his guide announced, breaking the awkward silence. "Girls, dinner's ready."

The scrape of chairs and young voices filled the room moments before a rush of bodies streamed out of the room. Murmurs of "hot," "Sydney's got game," and "day-aam" reached his ears. He bit back a smile and glanced at the woman next to him whom the girls greeted as Ms. Yolanda as they filed past. The corner of her mouth twitched as if trying to contain a smile.

When the last girl disappeared down the hall, Ms. Yolanda nodded, her attention shifting behind him. He didn't need to look behind him to know Sydney was there. Her signature honeysuckle-and-sun scent pronounced her arrival like a herald's trumpet. The fragrance, which he doubted he'd ever be able to smell again without associating it with her, reminded him of golden beams on equally bronzed skin. Of bare limbs tangling and crushing freshly mown grass, surrounded by a hedge of the lovely, fluted white flowers.

Of the sweet sin that was Sydney Blake.

"Sydney," Yolanda said, her direct stare remaining on him even as she addressed the other woman. Her unblinking scrutiny rested on his scar for a long moment, but unlike the rude ogling he was accustomed to, her open study didn't offend him. Possibly because she seemed to be cataloging his every feature in case she had to hunt him down later. "Have a good time tonight. It was nice meeting you, Mr. Oliver."

"She scares me," he drawled once the formidable older woman headed down the corridor and out of earshot.

"Yolanda?" Sydney snorted. "She and her sister, Melinda, are the youth center directors. Being in charge of anywhere between eight and one hundred teen girls at one time, she has to seem a little…um"—she chuckled softly—"daunting. But she loves the children, and they don't doubt it."

"Same with you," he murmured, finally turning to her. "They know they have your love, too."

An emotion glimmered in her eyes before her lashes lowered, hiding its identity from him. Anger, ignited by impatience and powerlessness, flared in his chest. She shouldn't be able to keep anything from him. Her thoughts, her emotions, even the loyalty she insisted on bestowing on an old man who didn't deserve it or her. He wanted every part of her—wanted her to give it to him…

And where had *that* come from? The fierce need to possess, to own. Claim.

One more second and he would be beating on his chest, grunting, "Me, Tarzan. You, motherfucking Jane."

Frowning, he jerked his chin in the direction of the empty classroom. "How long have you volunteered here?"

She shrugged a shoulder. "A couple of years."

"A couple of years?" he repeated. "I don't remember seeing the center included in the Blake family bio on the auction program." Not to mention when he'd investigated her at the instigation of his plan, he'd compiled a record of the boards and committees she sat on in case he could use the information to his advantage. Apparently, he'd missed one.

Again that…something…flickered in her gaze. And again it eluded him. "I suppose this isn't as sexy as the junior league."

He didn't know which surprised him more—the bite in

her voice or that he found the cutting wit hot as hell. In the end, though, the reason didn't matter. The fact that she did surprise him continued to confuse him, frustrated him. Set him on edge.

He stalked forward, and she edged back into the room, her contemplation of him turning wary, guarded. Then, as if realizing she'd retreated from him, she halted, tipped her chin up, and crossed her arms. The opposing gestures—one defiant, the other self-protective—struck him like an anvil. Strong yet fragile. Reserved yet tender. Courageous yet docile. Proud yet humble.

Determining the secrets of Area 51 would be easier than deciphering the mystery and dichotomies of Sydney Blake.

"You," he growled, shifting even closer, "are full of secrets."

She tilted her head, extended her hand. "Hello, pot," she drawled. "They call me kettle."

Lust rolled through him, a large bank of storm clouds struck by jagged bolts of need. Inhaling sharply, he cupped her face and swept his thumb under the plump curve of her bottom lip. He gripped her hip with his other hand, holding her steady…preventing her escape.

"Have I mentioned how much I adore your mouth?" he murmured. Her swift intake of breath urged him closer still. Provoked him to capture the gasp for his own, taste it with his tongue. "I do. It was one of the first things I noticed about you. Your pretty, wide, sexy-as-hell mouth. I've lain awake nights wondering…how would your lips feel on my skin? How would they look stretching for me, taking me? How much could you take?" Fire raced over his nerves, along his veins, turning him into the damn Human Torch. Needing a deeper, firmer touch, he pressed the tender flesh of her lip against the ridge of her teeth. Studied her for any sign of discomfort. And wondered if he would ease up or push her for more. "I've had your kiss. I know what you taste like, and that's only worsened the need. Made me crave more."

Their harsh breaths filled the room. This close, she couldn't hide behind her aloof facade. Couldn't conceal the desire darkening her eyes. Couldn't mask the flush across her patrician cheekbones. A low groan rumbled in his throat as he lowered his head…

"Is this your way of shutting me up, then?"

The cold, out-of-left-field accusation froze him faster than a January Chicago wind.

"What are you talking about?" he demanded, dropping his hand from her face as if burned.

Though the heat of arousal still stained her golden complexion, a distinct chill invaded her voice, as cutting as her words. "If I speak *out of turn*," she mocked, her lips twisted into a bitter caricature of a smile, "will you put me in my place with humiliating, vulgar talk? Shame me into being quiet?"

"First," he said, lowering his voice and allowing the throb of need in his cock to vibrate in his voice, "you can lie to yourself if it makes you feel better, but your body betrays you every time. You like my *vulgar talk*, sweetheart. Probably too much, which is why you're trying to verbally castrate me now. Understand one thing, though." He lowered his head until their noses bumped, and the soft, quick pants escaping her lips bathed his. The rigid length of his cock nudged her stomach, but he didn't retreat, didn't pretend like she didn't harden his body until he resembled a fucking statue. And she didn't back away, either. Her strength and stubbornness only stoked the flame inside him higher. "Yes, I can be ruthless, unforgiving, and a manipulative bastard. But I don't play games with sex."

It was one of the two areas in his life where he didn't lie—business being the other. He'd witnessed his mother exploiting her sexuality to control his father and other men too many times to ever use sex as a weapon or tool. There was no way she could comprehend how deeply that particular accusation cut.

"If I say I want you, then I want you. No lies, no ulterior motives. And, sweetheart…" He shifted back, dragged his gaze down the wet dream of her body deceptively clothed in a simple V-neck sweater and jeans. Shaking his head, he returned his eyes to hers. "I want to fuck you until neither one of us can move."

Chapter Nine

I want to fuck you until neither one of us can move.

The words spooled through Sydney's head like a never-ending reel. Or maybe her mind kept hitting repeat to hear the raw, erotic statement on a permanent loop in her head. Probably the former. She shifted on the black leather seat of the limo as a shiver coursed through her even nearly forty-five minutes after leaving the community center. Because in his blunt, I-don't-give-a-damn manner, Lucas had nailed the effect he had on her. The brutally honest admission of his lust and how he imagined them together— *How would they look stretching for me, taking me? How much could you take?*—had shaken her to the core. Literally. Her sex had fluttered, contracted, swelled as if preparing itself for what her brain stubbornly resisted. Even now, sitting in the limousine across from his large frame, inhaling his fresh scent with every breath, she ached with a nagging emptiness between her thighs.

Damn him.

Panic hurtled through her like a flash flood. Since ac-
quiescing to his blackmail, she'd been so certain she'd walk
away from this arrangement unscathed. That she could
portray the pleasant, content public face she'd learned to
maintain from the cradle. And in private, she could skate
through the year by continuing the two-ships-passing-in-a-
brownstone coexistence of the past week. She'd convinced
herself the kiss in his office had been an aberration, and that
sex with him would be the same as it'd been for her in the
past. Nice, but not that greedy, insane lust that had gripped
her whenever he was near her.

Bullshit.

Lucas hadn't even kissed her. Just touched her and
whispered in unadorned, explicit detail what he wanted.
Her. Under him. Over him. Shattered by his special brand
of pleasure.

And if she allowed herself to become lost to his brand of
consuming lust—let herself forget the cost—in a year's time,
that's exactly what she would be. Well and truly shattered.

Free of guilt. School. Autonomy. Freedom.

These were the things awaiting her once her year of in-
dentured service was up. As long as she kept them in mind,
she wouldn't waver. Wouldn't start to fall for the smoke and
mirrors called passion or love.

"I have something for you."

She jerked her attention from the window and the blur
of traffic to the enigmatic, sensual, and dangerous man shar-
ing her space. He'd lain aside the tablet he'd picked up as
soon as they'd entered the luxury vehicle, granting her first
easy breath since she'd glanced up to see him standing in the

doorway of the center's classroom. After years of being casually dismissed by her father in favor of business, she'd become accustomed to this kind of preoccupation. In a strange and admittedly dysfunctional way, the familiarity of his ignoring her had steadied her. But now that incisive turquoise gaze had refocused on her, the full impact of his personality and intensity behind it.

Hiking her composure before her like a shield, she arched an eyebrow in silent inquiry. His full lips tightened as if the gesture irritated him. Without releasing her from his scrutiny, he dipped his hand inside the interior pocket of his suit jacket. Seconds later, he extended his palm, and a small black box rested on the center.

Unable to control the fine tremble in her fingers, she plucked up the velvet case. An engagement ring. "Lucas, I—"

But a knot of emotion balled in her throat. She hadn't expected a ring, even though she should've, considering they would be married. But to her, the piece of jewelry represented commitment, unity, and respect. She might not have loved Tyler, but they had shared those values. She and Lucas had a contract signed in blackmail and ink.

Yet…

Yet as he opened the box, grasped her hand in a surprisingly gentle hold, then slid the ring onto her finger…the moment stole her breath away.

A large canary-yellow diamond cut in the shape of a rosebud bloomed from a cluster of smaller white diamonds and gold. Unlike Tyler's engagement ring—elegant, exquisite, and perfect for the socialite daughter of Jason Blake— this spoke of passion, life, of *her*. As if uppermost in his mind had been choosing a piece of jewelry she would love instead of selecting an ostentatious showpiece for the sake of oohs and ahs.

She blinked, stunned by the sudden sting of tears. *Stop it. It's silly to be moved by a ring when the engagement it represents is a farce.* So true. Now if only her stomach would quit executing backflips as if she'd just received a letterman's jacket from the high school football captain.

"Thank you," she whispered. "It's beautiful." *The most beautiful thing anyone's ever given me.* She curled her fingers as if trapping its heat...or preventing anyone from taking it from her.

"Yes, it is," he said softly. But those startling eyes weren't trained on the ring but her face. He lowered his head, freeing her from the brilliant captivity of his gaze. But when his lips opened over her hand, his tongue tracing the length of her ring finger, he tossed her into a new prison. One with bars of blazing need and a lock that could only be opened by the pleasure of his touch. She shivered, arousal winding through her veins like a slow-moving river on a hot summer day.

His dark, surprisingly soft hair fell on either side of his face, brushing her skin as he swirled his tongue around her fingertip, sucking lightly. *Jesus.* As if a thin wire connected her hand and her sex, each tug echoed between her legs, causing her flesh to swell, dampen. Deftly, he flipped her palm up and slowly placed an openmouthed kiss to the sensitive skin. She whimpered, squirming, trying to get away from the wicked caress...or get closer. His grip tightened, refusing to release her from the torture. The tip of his tongue traced invisible patterns, throwing kindling on the need burning in her stomach and lower. Good God. Who the hell would've known the tender skin between her fingers now receiving his attention were erogenous zones?

"It's just you and me here," she said, the words stumbling from between her lips and emerging as a halting pant. "You might want to save this kind of show for the gala, when we have an audience."

Lucas's lashes lifted, and she almost groaned at the hunger stamping his hard features. The thick, dark fall of waves and curls framed the sharp angles and planes of his face, emphasizing the desire burning in the turquoise stare that seemed to slice through the bullshit of her comment. Curling her fingers into a fist, she drew her arm back and convinced herself the flutter in her belly was irritation, not feminine excitement over the knowledge that he'd allowed her to withdraw. They both understood if he'd wanted to continue touching her, he would still be discovering new hot spots on her hand, like an erotic Lewis and Clark expedition.

Wearing a small half smile, he leaned back against the seat. The tiny smirk did nothing to detract from the sensual fullness of his lips. It did nothing to smother the arousal still blazing inside her. Instead she wanted to vault across the space separating them, straddle his hard thighs, and take his mouth. Conquer it. Tame it.

It was that almost overwhelming need that kept her pinned to her seat, throwing out verbal—and desperate—haymakers.

"That's the third time you've"—he paused—"put me in my place. News of your father's embezzlement, a broken engagement, marriage to me—those you take in stride without losing that damn icy Blake composure. But any mention of sex, any touch that isn't polite or nice 'n' neat, and your tongue turns into a Ginsu knife. What are you afraid of, Sydney? Sex?"

Sex? No, sex didn't terrify her. But what he made her feel—out of control, like a stranger in her own skin—that scared the hell out of her. What he would do to her body wouldn't be just sex. It would be something so much more explosive, wild, and raw. And afterward, he would leave her like a shipwreck survivor clinging to jagged rocks. Exhausted. Devastated. Lost.

"Of course not," she replied. "Did it ever occur to you that I don't like to be talked to like one of the women you date and discard? I'm supposed to be your fiancée, soon to be wife, not the current flavor of the month whose name you won't remember in the time it takes you to kick her out of the bed."

An eyebrow arched high. "And how would you know who I—how'd you put it—date and discard?" He planted a forearm on his leg and leaned forward, his steady contemplation gleaming with a bit of humor and something far darker. Hungrier. "Have you been doing your due diligence, sweetheart? Because any questions you have about my sex life I'll gladly answer."

She snorted. The devil probably bartered for someone's soul in that same alluring, seductive tone. "No, thanks. I believe I can live without those mental images."

His low chuckle slid under her dress and over skin like a soft caress. "To answer your question, yes, I did consider whether I would offend you." His gaze flicked down, skimming over the deep V-neck of the otherwise demure floor-length ruby-red gown. The intensity of his regard nearly singed her skin. And like a foolish moth to a deadly flame, she was drawn to that heat. "But then I noticed how your eyes soften, how your breath quickens, how your nipples harden. Aroused, sweetheart. That's what you get. Hot. I'd bet money on wet. But offended? Not. Even. Close," he growled. "And for the record, I don't have any mental images of the women before you. Every single memory has been replaced by fantasies of you in my bed, all those gorgeous curves bared for me, for my hands and cock. Of you taking me so deep, I won't want to find my way out of you."

"Stop…" she rasped, her core swelling, clenching, protesting the emptiness she instinctively knew only he could fill, satiate.

"You don't want my honesty. Something Tyler and the other men you've dated were too hypocritical, uptight, or scared to give you. They were thinking it, though, sweetheart. A man would have to be born without a dick to look at you and not want you."

Humiliation, anger, and sadness converged on her, his words dousing her with a rigid blast of realism and extinguishing the web of desire he so effortlessly wove.

"You're wrong," she stated, hurt pulsing in her chest like a homing beacon. "You like to demand I not pretend. Okay, I won't. So let's not *pretend* you want me for something other than my"—her lips twisted into bitter smile—"body. Let's not *pretend* I fit the mold of the women you're attracted to. Let's not *pretend* you're not just like the other men, just with far less pretty words. They were after money or my father's connections, and you're after revenge. No difference. Still cold. Still business."

Fury honed the angles of his face to sharply hewn stone, the scar bisecting his eyebrow a pale brand against taut skin. Before he could reply, the door to the limo opened, and the driver appeared. With a controlled grace that didn't conceal his rage, Lucas exited the vehicle. In that moment, she hated herself for drinking in the powerful build of his shoulders or the flexing of muscle under the black material of his pants.

When he turned back and extended his hand, he wore a pleasant, reserved mask. No hint of the anger that had suffused his features moments earlier. Resting her palm over his, she allowed him to draw her from the relative safety of the limousine.

Exhaling a deep, silent breath, she curved her lips into a perfect, gracious smile.

Let the charade begin.

• • •

The star and keynote speaker of the evening might have been a philanthropic New England Patriots football player, but the spotlight belonged to Lucas and Sydney. From the moment they entered the ballroom where the reception was held, the two of them had been the recipients of whispers, playful and sly innuendos, as well as covert and openly curious glances. Though she was no stranger to charity events and huge galas, being the center of such concentrated focus was alien to Sydney. Her father was the star of the Blake family, with her mother coming in second. She was the cog, the small piece that completed the wheel but that no one noticed. This…this constant speculation and attention crawled over her skin like an army of ants intent on lunch. And she was the main course.

"Stop fidgeting."

At the last second, she prevented herself from scowling

up at Lucas, recalling the avaricious attention fixed on them and recording every gesture, word, and look to gossip about later. "I don't fidget."

Playing the part of enamored fiancé to perfection, he lowered his head, pressing a kiss to the sleek hair she'd captured in a bun at the nape. The man deserved an Emmy for his performance in their little drama. "Yes, you are. You look beautiful and regal as always." The compliment ended in a low snarl as his lips grazed the top of her ear, the caress and words conveying an unbidden chorus of shivers down her spine. "But I swear to God, if one more asshole drools over your chest, I'm going fucking Chernobyl."

Startled, she glanced down at her dress. The deep V of the neckline revealed the inner curves of her breasts, but the high waist, three-quarter sleeves, and wide, flowing A-line skirt prevented the gown from edging into *What Not to Wear* territory. Lucas followed her gaze and his mouth tightened, his fingers flexing on her waist.

"While that might be fun to witness, I don't think it will ingratiate you in certain social circles," she said.

"You find my imminent explosion over some rude bastard funny?"

A corner of her mouth quirked. "A little."

And more than a little flattering and pleasurable, even though her brain argued his display of possessiveness was a superb act for the benefit of the other partygoers. Yet the knowledge didn't impede the somersaults in her stomach at each touch, each endearment, each brush of his mouth over her hair, forehead, or cheek. The heated looks and gestures might have been pretense on his part, but her reactions — the flocks of butterflies, the blushes, the delight — were all genuine. Her one saving grace was Lucas didn't know she wasn't as great an actor as he.

"Lucas." A gorgeous brunette in a silver and black mermaid-style dress only the truly thin could pull off glided up to them. Her long-lashed blue eyes flickered over Sydney before quickly dismissing her. Smiling up at Lucas, she settled a hand on his chest, her fingers stroking the lapel of his suit jacket. "I was hoping you would be here this evening."

"Hello, Caroline." He gently circled her wrist and lowered her arm. "Caroline, I'd like you to meet Sydney Blake, my fiancée. Sydney, this is Caroline Dresden. She owns several boutiques in Boston."

The other woman loosed a low, sensual laugh. "You make us sound like business associates, Lucas, when we're… friends." Neither the strategic pause nor the implied intimacy of "friends" was lost on Sydney. Her chest tightened as nausea roiled in her belly. "When I arrived, I heard the rumor that you were engaged, but I refused to believe it. I have to confess, this is certainly a surprise." Once more Caroline surveyed Sydney, cataloging every detail, and the slight smirk announced the woman found Sydney the surprise. "Sydney Blake," she murmured, tapping a fingertip against her lush bottom lip. "Jason Blake's daughter?"

"Yes." Sydney braced herself.

"Ah."

Translation: *It all makes sense now.* Anger and embarrassment wormed an insidious path through Sydney, burrowing in her heart. Of course this woman would believe who her father was could be the only reason a gorgeous, sensual man like Lucas would want Sydney. That the truth veered so close to her assumption tasted like ashes on Sydney's tongue.

In a feat that would've made Hercules go sit in a corner and suck his thumb, she managed to maintain her composure — no matter that it was as worn and tattered as an old shawl.

"Well, I guess congratulations are in order," Caroline said, wearing a satisfied, cat-who-ate-a-whole-damn-flock-of-canaries smile. "In deference to my friendship with Lucas, I would love for you to come by one of my boutiques. But I'm afraid my designs cater to less" — she paused — "Rubenesque women."

"Sheathe your claws, Caroline," Lucas snapped.

Too late. Her arrow had struck its target. And Caroline's hasty, conciliatory apology couldn't conceal her spite or her malicious joy. Pain radiated from inside Sydney, a mushroom cloud that seemed to expand with each razor-edged breath. Yes, she'd been on the receiving end of criticizing comments and backhanded compliments before. But this was different. This had been personal. Mean. And all because of the man standing next to her.

For the first time in her life, she thanked her mother for the poise she'd drummed into Sydney with tyrannical insistence. Drawing her shoulders back, Sydney nodded. "I appreciate your offer just the same," she murmured, voice steady, calm, not betraying one iota of the humiliation clawing at her chest. "It was a pleasure meeting you, Ms. Dresden. If you will excuse me."

Without waiting for Lucas's agreement or permission, she turned and waded through the heavy throng of guests, heading for the exit.

Her role in tonight's screwed-up performance was over. She quit.

Chapter Ten

"Sydney."

As Sydney crossed the threshold of the brownstone and entered the foyer forty-five minutes after leaving the charity benefit, Lucas's hard, firm tone demanded she stop, obey. An innate part of her wanted to yield, to submit to the unspoken order. But the other part—the hurt, angry, bruised part—silently told him and his kneel-before-Zod attitude to go suck it.

The rebellious side of her psyche won out. She didn't pause and continued toward the stairs and her temporary bedroom,

"Damn it, Sydney. Wait." A gentle but implacable grip halted her mid-step. She stiffened and wrenched her arm away from Lucas's, and he let her go. Still she seethed. What the hell? Hadn't he gotten the clue in the limo when he'd tried to talk to her, and she shut him down? What did he want from her? Hadn't being called fat by one of his former bedmates been enough entertainment for the evening? Rubenesque. Curvy. Statuesque. She'd heard them all—been called them all. And advice on amazing diet plans or offers of plastic surgeons' names who were positively brilliant with liposuction most often followed the clever euphemisms.

After years of the commentary on her body and weight, she should have skin as thick as an elephant's hide. Especially since her mother was author of a good portion of the remarks. But tonight had been vicious. And it'd occurred in front of Lucas.

Remnants of heat suffused her chest and face again.

"Yes?" She descended a step and faced him.

"Don't give me that lady-of-the-manor act," he snapped. "We need to talk about tonight."

Really? Talk about how they'd bumped into a woman who knew with disgusting intimacy how he looked naked? Not. Damn. Likely. "Okay. Obviously the news of our sudden engagement has made the rounds. But I think we did a little damage control with our appearance. You were very convincing as a man madly in love, which I think helped mitigate some of the gossip. Of course, I think we're going to need more than one evening to—"

"Stop it." He tugged her closer. "I don't give a damn about what people thought or didn't think."

"You should. As shallow as it may seem, some of them will decide whether or not to associate with you or your business because of this broken engagement. They'll judge you as impetuous or untrustworthy. That if your personal life is a reflection of how you run your company, they would rather not—"

"You're crawling back behind that ice queen facade you

consider a safety net. But I'm not letting you go so easily," he gritted out from between clenched teeth. "Why did you run?"

Outrage colored her vision until she viewed him through a misty crimson veil. "Run? So it's my fault your ex…whatever is a catty, ill-bred, rude — "

"Bitch. I believe that's the word you're dancing around," he supplied. "And no, I'm not blaming you for her behavior. But I want to know why you left as if you had something to be ashamed of. Have your parents ground you down to the point where you believe you deserve that kind of treatment?"

His questions struck too close. Much too close.

"What do you suggest I should've done?" She descended another step that brought her face-to-face with him. "Grab her by the hair? Roll around on the floor, scratching and punching? And what about the next time I meet someone you've been with? And the next time? And the next time? I might need to store boxing gloves in my purse if I'm going to throw down every time we come across a woman you've scratched an itch with."

She stormed past him, dragging her palms over her hair. Who was this woman throwing verbal low blows? She didn't recognize her — didn't like her. Resentment and helplessness mingled in the noxious brew already simmering in her stomach. She hated not being in control. Hated the emotions swirling and twisting inside her, making her weak, vulnerable, open to his incisive scrutiny.

In spite of the scandal their abrupt engagement had stirred, men had deferred to Lucas tonight, spoken to him with reverence and admiration. Women had stared at him, lusted after him. His sole worth wasn't tied to his name or the blood running through his veins. He commanded respect on his own merit and power. Her? She didn't even receive esteem or love from her own father. To both Jason and Lucas, she was an object. A pawn to be pushed around a chessboard by their motives and agendas.

"We can talk about how many women I've been with. We can talk about how some of them are faceless, and how I wish more of them were. We can talk about how I liked some of them and loved none of them." She pivoted and faced him where she'd left him, hands stuffed into the pockets of his pants, his hooded gaze fixed on her. "We can talk about all of that. Later. Right now I want an answer to my question. Because right now, it's everything I can do to remain standing here instead of going over to your father's house and wringing his ungrateful neck."

Lucas stalked closer, reminding her of a huge, dark jungle cat on the hunt. Common sense and self-preservation urged her to retreat, but experience warned her to stand her ground. Like any predator that smelled fear, he would press his advantage, exploit her weakness. The weakness being her body's traitorous response to his nearness, his scent. His words. His touch. Especially his touch.

"Why do I have the ugly suspicion you believe that bullshit he spouted in his office?" he asked.

She lowered her gaze to the strong column of his neck. At some point during the return ride home, he'd removed his tie and loosened the top button. Dusky, smooth skin stretched taut over the powerful jut of his collarbone, and she studied the sliver of flesh as if it contained all the nebulous answers to the universe. Anything to avoid meeting his stare that seemed to see too much, to peer too deep.

"Caroline only said what other people are thinking,"

she said softly. "That you're marrying me because of my last name, to get closer to my father and his connections." Inhaling, she lifted her head. And nearly reconsidered retreating in the wake of the turquoise fire blazing down at her. "Like me, they've probably seen the women you've dated. None of them look like"—she paused—"me. The charade of being in love is necessary, but not everyone will accept that your sudden affection isn't financially motivated." She squared her shoulders, tilted her chin higher. Pride might be regarded as a sin for the world, but for a Blake, it was a virtue. A necessity. And right now, it was all she had left. "Your goal is to humiliate my father personally and professionally. Mission halfway accomplished. By the time we marry next week, your vendetta against him will be realized. Does it matter who or what I believe? Will it change your mind about this engagement? This marriage?"

"No."

The immediate, harsh reply shouldn't have sucker punched the wind from her chest. Lucas had never lied to her about his plans and her role in them. The anger he possessed for her father veered toward hatred. His motivations exceeded money or social acceptance. What? Had she expected he would abruptly abort his campaign for revenge and blackmail because of her feelings? She almost loosed a bark of laughter. That would require placing her desires, her needs, her heart ahead of his own agenda. And no one—not even her parents—had ever done that.

"Good night, Lucas." She turned toward the staircase, suddenly tired. The weight of his scrutiny propelled her across the foyer, incited a desperation to escape it. Tomorrow, when the veneer over her emotions didn't stretch so thin as to be damn near transparent, she could face him again. But not tonight…

A hard, solid wall of muscle smacked against her back, driving the breath from her lungs. Only the unyielding band of a black-sleeved arm prevented her from pitching forward. Heat licked against her spine and neck.

"You're right," Lucas murmured in her ear, the almost gentle tone at complete odds with the arm anchoring her waist …and the rigid, thick erection branding her through layers of clothes. She sank her teeth into her bottom lip, battling back a groan and the prurient desire to grind against the steely length. "I've never been with a woman like you. They're faceless, nameless, insignificant, while you? I can't exorcise you from my mind. Sweetheart, sex has been good before, but nothing like the damn near primal need that has been riding me day and night. And I haven't even been inside you yet. One kiss, Sydney. One kiss. I haven't felt you tremble under me, haven't had your arms and legs wrapped around me. But damn, do I want it. No, don't do that," he murmured. Softening his hold on her waist, he placed his thumb on her lip and eased it from beneath her teeth. "There you go." He hummed, rubbing the slight tenderness from her flesh. "Let me…"

He slowly tunneled his fingers under her bun, maybe giving her time to push him away or step out of his embrace. Her carefully styled hair started to loosen and unravel as his blunt nails grazed her scalp, and he gently pulled her head back. This time, she couldn't contain the moan. It slipped free of its own will.

"I love that sound coming from you. Is that what you were trying to hold back from me?" He smoothed another caress over the lip she'd closed her teeth over. "Why? When this"—he brushed a kiss over the corner of her mouth—"is the only honesty we have between us."

He tugged her head back farther and covered her mouth with his. His hand returned to her chin, keeping her steady for the plunge of his tongue. While his grip might've been devastatingly tender and sensual, the kiss wasn't. He didn't cajole or tease playfully. He took. And God, she gave. Surrendered. Submitted. When his tongue coiled around hers, demanding she do the same, she did. When he squeezed her jaw and slowly thrust in and out, mimicking how his cock would stroke her sex, she shuddered and let him. And when he angled his head and muttered, "Open wider," before sweeping deeper, claiming more, she obeyed.

A faint ache pulsed along her neck as he bent her head back even farther. But she didn't resist, didn't whimper a protest. Because then he would stop drowning her in the most wicked, blistering desire she'd ever experienced. Then a cool draft blew over, combating the fire.

Startled, she opened her eyes. Met his sensual, hooded stare.

More air bathed her shoulders, her chest, her…breasts. *Oh, God.* "Wait," she breathed, struggling in his embrace.

"Shh," he soothed, his lips skimming along her jaw. "Easy."

No, she couldn't… His big, warm hands closed over her bared breasts. Cupped them. Lust struck her like a lightning bolt, sizzling along her veins and crackling between her weak legs.

"Lucas," she whimpered, arching into his hands, grinding her head against his shoulder. She clawed at his arms, cuffed his wrists, uncertain. She should drag his hands away from her, but the purely sexual animal inside her held him to her flesh. Dared him to stop. "Please."

Please don't. Please don't stop. She couldn't voice what she didn't know.

But he seemed to understand what her mind and body warred against and came down firmly on the side of her libido. With another of those sexy growls that caused her belly to tighten and quiver, he shaped her, molded, squeezed. She didn't have time to be embarrassed over the weight of her C cups. Not when his hands enveloped her with such ease and reverence. His thumbs swept across the stiff, aching points of her nipples, and pleasure screamed through her like high-velocity winds. She groaned as her core, wet and needy, clamped down on a phantom cock that wasn't there to fill her.

"So sensitive," he praised, the rumble a rough caress over her skin. "And pretty. Goddamn, you're so pretty." He circled the hard tips, plucked and pinched them until she squirmed in his arms. Desperate for a harder touch, a deeper touch, she closed her hands over his, commanding him to give her more. His low chuckle echoed in her ear. "Can you come from just my hands on your breasts and nipples, Sydney?" He tweaked the buds, and she cried out, shuddering. "I think you can. What about my mouth, too? Come apart for me, Sydney."

Come apart. Come. Apart.

Her flesh cried out a resounding "hell, yes" at the silken, erotic invitation, but her heart, her brain shouted a blaring warning. Because if she did—if she came apart—what would be left? They weren't even married yet, and already she was surrendering to the very thing she'd vowed not to allow happen. Not sex—she'd agreed to sex in the marriage bed. But her emotions, her passion. She'd promised herself she'd walk away from this arrangement with her soul intact.

Not tonight. She couldn't give in when she was already hurting and vulnerable from the evening. Tonight she wasn't strong enough to wake up in his bed with her defenses intact.

"No," she rasped, infusing all her fear and confusion into a final shove. A second later, his arms fell from around her, freeing her. Surprising her.

She didn't question his immediate acquiescence, just took advantage of it. With fumbling fingers, she yanked her dress up over her shoulders, covering her flesh. She didn't turn around, afraid if she spied the hunger stamped on his taut features, she would change her mind and let him cast her into an abyss of pleasure that would leave her stripped and lost.

An image of her mother wavered and solidified. Not Charlene's cool, blond beauty, but the painful yearning and bitter acceptance as she stared after her father's retreating back. Yearning because her mother adored him. Bitterness because she knew the "business meeting" he was headed to would involve the newest young plaything he was cheating with. If Sydney didn't guard her heart, in a year she would become a perfect reflection of her mother—hardened, angry, and longing for a man who didn't love her.

"I'm sorry," she whispered, scrabbling for the banister. "I can't."

Then she fled up the stairs.

Fled from him.

Fled from the consuming passion he ignited in her.

Fled from herself.

Chapter Eleven

Sydney inhaled. Exhaled. Did it again.

Nope.

Her heart still pounded in her chest like a captive wild thing.

Her wedding day.

Oh, God. She grasped the gleaming banister and contemplated the curving flight of stairs leading from the second level like it had transformed into a booby-trapped maze straight out of an Indiana Jones film. And she had to traverse it in less than sixty seconds to meet her groom.

Her groom. The man she would pledge her body, heart, and fidelity to. The man who had coerced her into a devil's bargain called marriage. The man who would force her to lie in front of friends and a man of the cloth.

They were both going to hell.

Below her the beautiful opening notes of Bach's Cello Suite No. 1 danced in the air. Her cue to descend the steps and begin the walk down the aisle. Her belly did another roll and dive.

You can do this. You've come this far. You're doing this for your father, and he's worth it.

Sucking in another deep breath, she began her bridal march down the staircase. The dull roar in her ears almost drowned out the music as she neared the entrance to the brownstone's great room. The space had been cleared of furniture and transformed into a makeshift chapel, complete with ribboned chairs on either side of the aisle for their thirty or so guests, tall candelabra and flowers. A white runner had been rolled down the middle of the aisle, leading her to her soon-to-be husband like the yellow brick road guided Dorothy to the Emerald City.

Clutching her small bouquet—strangling it, really—she risked a glance in the room. And her heart thumped in a sharp leap of joy. Her father and mother sat in the front row. She hadn't spoken to either of them since she'd left home, but they'd come.

Oh, Jesus. Moisture fled from her mouth, and butterflies evacuated her stomach to make room for raptors. *What am I doing? I can't go through...*

She lifted her head and spotted him for the first time.

The birds in her stomach settled. The room and people disappeared, her world falling into an expectant hush.

His turquoise gaze locked with hers—and refused to let go. A curious melting started in her chest and wound its way through her. She should be angry, resentful, terrified—any range of emotions. Instead, as she put one foot in front of the other and started down the aisle toward this impossibly handsome, scarred man who waited for her with quiet intensity, an emotion she couldn't identify—was too scared to identify—filled her.

And when he extended his hand toward her, she didn't hesitate when she placed hers in his.

She didn't trust him. Didn't love him. Didn't really know him. But at this moment, she couldn't picture meeting any-one else but him at the end of the runner.

Ah. There was the terror, after all.

The short ceremony rushed by at lightning speed. Soon, the reverend asked them to repeat after him. She didn't stumble over her vows, and to her ears she sounded truthful.

Almost over. We're almost there.

"Lucas has prepared special vows for his bride," the pastor announced with a nod.

Sydney barely controlled her flinch of surprise. He had? Why? This wasn't a usual, loving ceremony. Why would he…?

"Sydney," he began, his deep timbre at once loud and intimate, almost as if for her ears only. "I know our relation-ship has been…unconventional. I know your acceptance of me and us has been a sacrifice and a leap into the un-known. I promise today, in front of family and friends, that you haven't leaped alone. And from this day forward, for as long as we are together, I vow you will never be alone again. I promise to protect you, provide for you, shelter you, and dedicate every day of our marriage proving to you how beautiful and special you are. How wanted you are."

Tears, unbidden and hot, stung her eyes. To their wed-ding guests, she probably appeared like an emotionally overcome bride touched by her groom's pledge of love. But they didn't understand the hidden truth. This…this message wrapped up in pretty words actually meant something to her—where the traditional vows wouldn't have—because they were honest. No promises of love and until death do us part. Just his own promise to honor her. To respect her.

And for the year they would be man and wife, it was enough.

"Lucas." She paused, but the flash of surprise and maybe even pleasure in his eyes encouraged her to continue. "You were…unexpected in my life." She couldn't help the small smile at the private meaning between the two of them. "I promise today that I will be the wife you need and won't betray you. And for as long as we are together, you won't walk alone, either."

She held out the ring she'd clutched in her hand.

"With this ring, I thee wed."

• • •

He was a married man.

Even as Lucas accepted more congratulations from one of the guests invited to the intimate ceremony, he sought out the woman responsible for the simple but elegant transformation of his brownstone's parlor level into a wedding venue.

Sydney Blake. Sydney Oliver, now.

His wife.

Vibrant red, orange, and gold leaves outside the floor-to-ceiling bay windows created a brilliant backdrop for his bride as she chatted with Terry Henley, the CFO of Blake Corporation and her godfather. Shoulders Lucas had bared and kissed just seven days ago gleamed like honey. The strapless lace and silk dress cupped her breasts and waist then flowed over her hips, ending in a train. Her thick caramel-colored strands looped and swirled around her head into a loose tail that appeared soft…romantic.

Gorgeous as hell.

Grim resolve settled in his chest like a great boulder in a dark, bottomless well. He'd plotted, threatened, and blackmailed to voluntarily shackle himself in a commitment he detested.

But Lucas wasn't blinded by love and denial. This union had a single purpose. And though he wanted—fucking lusted—after his wife with a need that bordered on insanity, he'd let her walk away a year from today. Before he'd put this plan into place, he hadn't planned on getting married. His experience had taught him that love, honesty, and fidelity were elusive dreams when money, power, or prenups were involved. And while Sydney hadn't married him for who he was or what he possessed, blackmail didn't make a solid foundation for marriage, either.

"For a man who just entered connubial bliss, you don't look very happy."

Lucas shot a glance at Aiden, who'd appeared at his elbow. "Shut it."

His friend shrugged and sipped from a glass of champagne. "Sydney did a beautiful job. Especially considering what she had to work with. You know, time constraints, last-minute details…blackmail."

"Aiden," Lucas growled.

"Fine, fine," he drawled, his free hand held up in surrender. "Those were beautiful vows."

Aiden arched an eyebrow as if waiting for a response or explanation from him. Lucas stared at his friend, silent. Aiden would be waiting there for a long damn time before he received one. Not when Lucas couldn't even explain to his own self why he'd written them the night before. Hell, he didn't want to analyze why.

Nor did he dwell on how the vows Sydney had declared in return had rocked him to his core.

"Okay, I'll back off since it's your wedding day." Aiden surveyed the room, a frown drawing down his dark blond eyebrows. "I thought you said Sydney's father disowned her," he murmured. "But he's here."

Yes, Jason and Charlene had attended the wedding. They'd even plastered on their fake smiles and appeared delighted in their daughter's choice of husband.

"I'd like to believe their motives are altruistic, but somehow I can't quite convince myself," Lucas drawled.

"Hmm." Aiden fell quiet for a moment, switching his thoughtful regard to Sydney. "At least she seemed happy they showed up. I guess that's all that matters. No bride should be upset on her wedding day."

True, pleasure had sparkled in Sydney's eyes when she'd spied them as she descended the staircase and entered the large living room. That moment when her face had lit up with a lovely, genuine smile—not that hated, aloof, cold caricature she usually wore—had been worth the knowledge that her parents had most likely decided to attend to save the untarnished image of a perfect family, not for her sake.

"Speak of the devil… I think your new father-in-law wants a word with you." Tension invaded Aiden's tall frame and hardened his features. Most people witnessed the affable, easygoing playboy and rarely met the man honed to razor sharpness by the cruel and pitiless Chicago streets. "You need me to stay?" he asked as Jason strolled toward them, pausing to greet guests as if he were the host and proud father of the bride.

The fury and hatred that always simmered beneath the surface surged, hot and fierce, scalding Lucas. Jason had that effect on him. "No, I'm fine," he said, voice flat. "Thank you, though." He clapped a hand to Aiden's shoulder.

"Okay." He lifted his glass for another sip, but his regard, narrowed and glittering, remained on Jason. "I'll be over there charming your wife."

Lucas snorted before inhaling and turning to face the man who'd given Lucas's life purpose—retribution.

His new wife's father.

"Lucas." Jason's loud, jovial greeting grated his ears. Particularly when one look into the other man's ice-cold hazel eyes revealed a loathing that rivaled his own. "Congratulations, and welcome to the family, son." He pumped Lucas's hand, pulling him close for a quick, hard embrace even as Lucas's stomach rebelled at "son." He hoped to hell he had lye in the kitchen. Mere soap and water wouldn't scrub away the thick, grimy coat of Jason's duplicity.

"I'm glad you and your wife could make it, Mr. Blake," he said smoothly.

"We wouldn't have missed Sydney's big day for the world. As long as she's happy, we are, too. And none of this Mr. Blake nonsense. We're family now. Please, call me Jason." Jesus Christ, the man should run for office with all the bullshit he was slinging. Jason inclined his head. "Would you mind if I tear you away from the party for a moment? There's something I would like to speak with you about. Privately."

"Of course," Lucas murmured. Feeling the weight of the interest on the two of them, he led Jason from the living room and down the stairs to the garden level of the brown-stone that he'd had converted to a study, home office, and library. He strode over to the fully stocked bar. "Can I pour you a drink, Jason?"

"Cut the crap, Oliver," the other man snapped.

Sighing, Lucas tipped a finger of bourbon into a tumbler and recapped the decanter. "I suppose it's safe to say the pleasantries are over?" he mocked.

"I've been busy since you and Sydney showed up at my office with your little *announcement*." He spat the last word, distaste twisting his handsome features. "Raised in the South Side of Chicago by Duncan Oliver, your construction worker uncle. Paid your way to the University of Chicago by working on those construction sites beside him. Graduated summa cum laude in three years with a bachelor's degree in finance and in another two years, earned an MBA. Started your business at the age of twenty-one. Bought your first company under the Bay Bridge Industries umbrella at twen-ty-four. Earned your first million at twenty-five. A brilliant and formidable businessman. A real rags-to-riches story that makes wonderful copy."

Lucas didn't reply as Jason ticked off the facts of his per-sonal and professional life that could be found in any com-pany brochure or newspaper article. The darker details of his history had been carefully hidden under so many layers of lies, documentation, and greased palms, Jason would've had to hire Sherlock Holmes to ferret out the truth behind Lucas's identity. Still…unease curled in his gut. He didn't put anything past this man.

"Isn't that what makes our country so wonderful?" Lu-cas studied Jason over the rim of his glass. "All a man has to do is work hard with integrity and determination, and he can accomplish all of his dreams." Like Lucas's father, Jason had inherited his wealth. But unlike Robert Ellison, Jason hadn't been satisfied until he'd stolen his best friend's reputation, money, and wife to compound that wealth. Integrity? What Jason knew of that concept could be stuffed into a gnat's ass with room to spare. "Am I supposed to be ashamed of my past?"

"A boy born to nothing always hungers for more. The thing about that boy is he eventually becomes a man with the same insatiable hunger for better, to be better. And where breeding can't get him, he'll use money or people."

Lucas sipped the amber alcohol and welcomed the burn over his tongue and down his throat. It distracted him from the rage-fueled pain that had taken root in every organ so it pumped through his blood, infiltrated his arteries, escaped him with every breath.

"And Sydney would be the person I'm using to infiltrate the rarefied stations I could never obtain on my own because my blood is red instead of blue, is that it?" The fucking irony.

"Don't misunderstand me, Oliver," Jason growled, stalking closer, fists tight at his sides. "No matter how long my family has lived in Beacon Hill…no matter that Blake Corporation has been in existence for decades, and its subsidiaries have provided employment to not just this city but the country…no matter how many zeroes are on the bottom line of my P&L statements…to some people, I will be nothing more than a black man worthy to shine their shoes but not darken their doorsteps. So I have nothing against your background. But that doesn't mean *you* don't." He jabbed a finger at Lucas. "There's a chip on your shoulder big enough to break a man's back. And while my daughter may think she's in love, I don't want her to end up a casualty of your ambition. She's been hurt enough." A fleeting dark emotion flashed through his eyes. "Suffered enough. I won't let you use her."

Shock momentarily banked the fire blazing inside him.

"I hate to disappoint you, but if you think marrying me will hurt my father, you're sorely mistaken…ultimately, one wealthy, connected son-in-law will be just as fine as another."

Sydney's warning from a couple of weeks ago haunted him. Apparently, she'd been wrong. Her father did care. Or he deserved one hell of an award for best performance by a concerned father. With Jason Blake, he couldn't tell.

"So disowning your daughter was your way of not hurting her?" Lucas set the tumbler on the bar and crossed his arms, eyebrow arched. "Taking away the only family she has is your idea of not inflicting suffering?"

Jason's lips curling back from his teeth in a snarl. "Don't dictate to me what's best for Sydney. If that was the only way to prevent her from making this mistake, then I would do it again. But I'm here today, aren't I? And this isn't over." He strode closer until Lucas could spy the thin lines radiating from Jason's eyes, the deeper ones bracketing his mouth. "I don't trust you. Those people out there—your business colleagues, friends, my daughter—you may have them fooled, but you're after something, and it isn't Sydney's hand in marriage. If you truly had her best interests at heart, you would've left her alone, let her marry Tyler. Have a good life."

Slowly, Lucas lowered his arms and straightened from his sprawl against the bar top. "And Reinhold would've made her happy? She would've had a good life by whose standards? Yours? You don't know your daughter, Jason."

The anger returned, bright and searing. "Did she want that marriage? Or did *you*?" When the older man didn't reply, but his mouth firmed into a grim line, Lucas nodded. "I won't betray Sydney. I won't ignore her, neglect her. I didn't marry her to hurt her."

He wouldn't dress her up in stylish clothes, parade her around like a show horse, and then stable her until he needed her again. That was the life Jason had intended to condemn his daughter to—the life Sydney had agreed to. No, Lucas didn't love her; if not for his hatred and plans for Jason, he wouldn't have married her. Still, she was a vibrant, beautiful, sensual woman who deserved to be seen for herself, not her family name or blood. With Tyler, she would've eventually paled into a blurred gray version of the woman who'd grabbed Lucas by the neck and demanded his fidelity. The woman who patiently and willingly devoted her time and love to teen girls. The woman who'd writhed with passion in his arms.

The thought of Tyler possessing and squandering all that fire had his fist clenching until an ache pulsed across his knuckles. No, more than his next breath, he wanted to taste that desire, be consumed by her fire.

"Forgive me if I don't take your word for it," Jason retorted, and with one last fulminating glare, pivoted and stalked from the room.

Lucas finished his drink and moments later followed, his vow about not hurting Sydney reverberating against his skull.

Too bad he couldn't still the small voice inside his head warning him that by ruining her father, he would be inflicting the worst damage of all.

Chapter Twelve

Sydney Oliver.

Her new name. Or at least it would be for the next year.

Sinking to the living room couch, she removed first one high heel, then the other. With a groan, she rubbed her thumb into the sole, massaging away the dull ache caused by hours on her feet. And as long as she concentrated on her sore feet, she could keep the thoughts of her new husband at bay.

Panic mingled with tendrils of excitement, and she paused mid-rub, bowing her head. Panic because tonight he probably expected her to share his bed. And excitement because he probably expected her to share his bed.

"You're demanding fidelity, and I'll give you that. But if I intended to be celibate, I would've become a priest."

She shivered as memories of the last time Lucas had touched her flooded her brain like a faucet that had been twisted on. The images poured into her brain. His big hands on her flesh. His dark, sensual voice in her ear. His hard body pressed to hers. *Jesus.* Arousal pounded like an anvil against metal, and suddenly the corset beneath her dress was cinched too tight. The soft silk and lace too harsh on her sensitized skin. Her panties not substantial enough against the liquid heat building between her thighs.

A week ago, she'd believed she would be ready for this — for him. Seven days with limited contact and the most cursory communication with Lucas had instilled a false sense of confidence and security that, yes, she could consummate this marriage. *Consummate.* She huffed out a breath. Such an innocuous word for something so…cataclysmic.

"The last guest left?"

She glanced up as Lucas entered the room. And quickly returned her attention to her sore feet. But too late. His image was already branded on her retinas. Tousled dark hair falling around his lean face. Jacketless. White dress shirt opened at the collar, sleeves rolled up to reveal strong, muscled forearms. Large, bare feet. Why did the sight of his feet impact her the most? The intimacy of it? The…vulnerability of it?

So not fair. They were feet, for God's sakes. There was nothing sexy about toes…

Unless they were attached to Lucas Oliver, apparently.

"Yes," she replied, realizing she hadn't answered his question. "About ten minutes ago. Did your call work out okay?" He'd received a phone call about half an hour before the end of the reception. Business, since he'd disappeared. The knot in her chest had been irritation, not disappointment. Because it wasn't as if their marriage was real instead of a trade discussed and signed off on in a corporate office.

Actually, his conducting business on their wedding day was the most honest transaction of the day.

"Fine." He leaned a shoulder against the wall, arms crossed, one ankle propped over the other. Head cocked to the side, he studied her. Even though she kept her head bowed, she sensed his turquoise scrutiny, felt it like a tactile trail of fingers over her hair, shoulders, collarbone. The tops of her breasts. "Sydney," he murmured.

"Yes?"

"Today was beautiful. The house, the ceremony, the reception—everything was wonderful. Thank you."

She straightened, stunned by him for the second time that day. "Thank you" she heard often enough for work on a committee or a donation to one cause or another. But praise? Compliments? Only at the youth center, where they appreciated her, valued her. Almost never anywhere else, including home, where her efforts were her duty, expected.

"I—" She shook her head. "You're welcome."

"Would you like me to do that for you?" When she frowned, he nodded at her foot.

"N-no," she stammered. Touch her? God, no. "I'm okay. Earlier, I saw you leave with Dad," she said, hurriedly changing the subject from his hands on any part of her body. "Is everything okay? What did he want to talk with you about?"

The corner of his mouth hitched in a small smirk. "He doesn't trust me."

She laughed, the sound brittle and sharp. "Yes, well, after my mother pulled me aside for a heart-to-heart during the reception, I figured out pretty quick why they decided to make an appearance today." And it had been an appearance. A cameo. A show.

"Why?" Lucas straightened from his sprawl against the wall, the movement languorous, his eyes hooded, dangerous.

"Why did they come, or why did she pull me aside?"

"Both. Either."

"They attended to show our family *solidarity*. Still, she wanted to make sure I fully comprehended the damage my immature and impetuous decision—her words—caused them. How I'd humiliated both of them and harmed not just Dad's professional relationship with the Reinholds but their personal one, as well. She didn't understand how she could've raised such a selfish daughter and not realized it."

Pain radiated from inside her, eclipsing the numbness she'd enveloped her feelings in for the duration of the gathering. Burying the hurt and disappointment had been the only way she could return to the party and smile, chat, and laugh as if she were the happiest of brides. But now, repeating the accusations, they cut into her heart like dozens of tiny slices.

"Selfish?" Lucas rumbled. "Bullshit. What did you say to her?"

"What could I say, Lucas? 'Mom, I broke off my engagement to a man I dated for over a year to marry a man I barely know so Dad doesn't go to jail.'" She splayed her hands wide, palms up. "'I hope you understand.'" Again, she chuckled, and it was as bitter and hard as its predecessor. "I don't know what you want from me. Tonight, at the gala last week. What do you want?"

"You to tell them all to go to hell," he growled. Leaning down, he extended his hand, palm out. After a long hesitation, she placed hers in his, and he pulled her to her feet. He tugged her across the room to a gilt-framed mirror hanging on the wall. Drawing her in front of him, he cupped her chin and made her stare at their reflection. "Impetuous? Immature?" His soft tone belied the anger in the blue-green stare blazing back at her from the glass. "This woman is the most conscientious, selfless, considerate person I've met. And I've known her for weeks. How do they not recognize it? And why does she let them get away with not acknowledging it? With not respecting her gifts, her heart, her feelings?"

Because she owes them! Sydney almost cried out. Her teeth sank into her bottom lip, trapping the admission.

"No." He touched his thumb to her lip and gently but firmly tugged it free. "I told you not to do that."

He rubbed her flesh, and she helplessly stared at the sensual picture they created. His big body covered her back and shoulders. His dark head bent over hers. His thumb soothing her mouth as his other hand splayed wide over her abdomen. Her muscles contracted hard, the erotic ache echoing in the deepest, emptiest part of her.

"Lucas," she breathed, reaching up and circling his wrist. "I can't."

"Can't what?"

His eyes refused to free her as his hand rode higher on her torso, his thumb coming to rest between her breasts. The caress on her mouth emboldened, pressed instead of brushed. The more insistent touch sensitized her breasts, tingled in her nipples, resonated and throbbed in her sex.

She tightened her grip on his wrist.

"This," she rasped. "What you expect of me. Tonight. I just—can't."

He stilled behind her, tension nearly vibrating against her skin, humming in the air around them.

"Why?" he finally asked. "Are you going to say you don't want it?" As if daring her to utter the untruth, he dragged the pad of his thumb over the tip of her breast. The flesh pebbled, begging for another stroke. A harder one.

"No." She briefly lowered her lashes, fumbled for any reason other than the truth. In spite of the special vows he'd uttered, the ceremony had been a lie. Her new last name was a lie. And now her wedding night would be one. When she stood here so emotionally raw, stripping her body bare before him, too, on a night that should have commemorated something beautiful and special seemed the biggest lie of all. He would find her sentiment foolish and misplaced, since her body cried out for his in a way that would make a banshee mute. But after sacrificing so much today, this one thing, this one night was the only thing she had control of. And she couldn't hand over one more piece of herself.

Not tonight.

"No," she repeated softly. "I'm not going to lie about my…attraction toward you. But not two weeks ago I was engaged to another man. I'm not breaking our contract, I'm just asking for time."

A taut, heavy silence as stifling and leaden as an ominous bank of clouds hung in the room. The weight of it— the threat of the imminent crash of the storm behind it— weighed on her skin.

"Are you still in love with him?"

"No." She'd *never* been in love with him.

Lucas's hands fell away from her. He shifted back, and the space relieved and distressed her. Jesus, she needed to get a grip.

His brooding gaze met hers in the mirror, the stark

outline of his scar lending his lean, sharp features even more of a menacing appearance.

She waited, breath trapped in her lungs, for his objection. For his demand she honor her part in this agreement.

"Sleep well, Sydney," he murmured, then turned and exited the room.

Leaving her more confused and lonely than ever.

Chapter Thirteen

Lucas thrust open the door to Sydney's room, not bothering with a warning knock. After a sleepless night, civility and manners had gone the way of sinners and that annoying Bieber kid's career: to hell. Besides, she'd asked him not to touch. She hadn't issued a stipulation about looking. Clenching his jaw, he shut the door on that train of thought and padlocked it for good measure. Just contemplating why she'd pushed him away last night…and for *whom*…

Yeah. Letting it go.

Early morning sunlight streamed in through the bay windows, gliding over the chaise lounge under the windowsill, across the hardwood floor, and onto the bed and rumpled blankets.

Where Sydney slept like some Disney princess under a curse.

He snorted. Why shouldn't she sleep soundly? She didn't have balls to turn so blue all they needed were white hats to look like fucking Smurfs.

Feeling like a Peeping Tom but unable to scrounge up a regret, he neared the bed. The pale yellow blankets twisted around her hips, and one of the long pillows had fallen to the floor. Satisfaction rolled through him with the subtlety of a freight train. *Good.* Maybe her night hadn't been as restful as he believed. Bending down, he picked up the pillow and propped it against the headboard. This close to her, that damn honeysuckle scent wrapped around him like chains. He'd bet the sheets smelled like her.

Hell, *he* wanted to smell like her.

Cursing, he reached for her shoulder and noticed the gray T-shirt with a red *B* and *U* blazoned across her breasts. His eyebrows jacked high. Sydney had always struck him as the forties-silky-nightgown type, not worn-old-college-shirt-and-boxers type. If she wore boxers. Great. Now exactly *what* lay under the blankets would bug him until he found out.

Muttering beneath his breath, he reached for her once more—and once more drew up short. He frowned. There was something different...

Her lashes fluttered, opened. Hazel eyes clouded with sleep peered up at him, soft and dreamy. Frozen, he stared, spying the almost smile as it touched her lips. Then noting the moment realization entered that lovely gaze and the curve inverted. Comprehension swept away the drowsiness, and she went rigid before scrabbling to a sitting position. The covers dropped farther down her hips, and he glimpsed red-and-black plaid. Again amusement trickled through confusion. Because he still couldn't figure out what had struck him as so odd...

"What are you doing in here?" she blurted, shoving her dark gold and brown curls out of her face.

Curls. Jesus. The wild tumble of long, dense spirals brushed her shoulders, forming a sexy halo around her beautiful features. The straight, perfectly styled strands belonged to the socialite. But these vibrant, untamed, *free* curls belonged to the woman.

"What the hell happened to your hair?" he demanded, shock and hot desire roughening his voice.

Embarrassment flashed across her face, flushing her cheekbones. "I showered last night and didn't have a chance to straighten it before you burst in my room *uninvited* at"— she glanced at the clock radio on the bedside dresser— "seven o'clock in the morning," she finished through gritted teeth. "I repeat, what are you doing in here?"

"Get dressed," he said, still off-kilter by this side of Sydney. Comfy, this-side-of-ratty pajamas, hair like a lion's mane… "We're leaving for our honeymoon in an hour."

She gaped at him. "Honeymoon? What are you talking about? I didn't think we were—"

"Well, we are." He'd decided to leave Boston and get away just last night. Cooped up in this house with her for the duration of the honeymoon and not be able to touch her? He'd lose his damn mind. "Pack enough for a week."

Flinging the blankets off, she scooted off the bed, and as she turned, worn cotton pulled tight across her breasts. *Oh, fuck. Me.* He clenched his jaw. Balled his fingers into fists.

"You can't just order me to pack for seven days and expect me to be ready in an hour," she protested, snatching up a short royal-blue robe off the chaise lounge. Clearly flustered, she speared her thick curls with her fingers. "I have to do my hair—"

"Leave it," he ordered. Her gaze snapped to his, wide, bemused. Inhaling, he deliberately softened the harsh edge to his demand. "Leave it." Pause. "Please."

Not waiting for her acquiescence, he strode from the room before he broke his promise not to touch her.

• • •

"I don't know what I was expecting. A high-rise condo in New York. A sunny California beach. But not this." Hair blowing in the brisk Puget Sound wind that swept the patio of his Bainbridge Island cabin—such a misnomer for the huge structure that could easily sleep about ten people but still managed to maintain its coziness—Sydney tossed him a smile over her shoulder. "It's beautiful, Lucas."

Lucas nodded and pressed a cup of freshly brewed coffee into her hands, his vocal cords momentarily frozen by the sight of that smile. Relaxed, sweet, unguarded. Since they'd met, he'd most often been the recipient of the polite, aloof turn of lips and the tight go-to-hell version. The one time he'd witnessed the delighted, open grin had been during their first dinner together.

Damn. How could he miss something he'd only had once?

"Thank you." He lifted his own mug and sipped, welcoming the fragrant brew that combated the brisk, rapidly cooling wind snapping off the dark waters surrounding Bainbridge Island. With dusk rolling in like a kid sprinting home before the streetlights came on, the warm Indian summer weather they'd enjoyed since arriving in Washington

State several hours earlier waved so long for the day. Yet she continued to stand at the patio railing, bundled up in a thick cream cable-knit sweater, tight jeans that made his cock whine like a little girl, and knee-high riding boots. "Are you sure you don't want to go inside? Dinner's almost ready." As Lucas had exited the house, his chef had been placing the finishing touches on a roast duck, and the delicious aroma had followed him outside.

"A few more minutes?" She tasted her coffee and hummed, her lashes lowering as she savored it. He stared at her mouth, at the pleasure softening her face, and turned away. He either had to stop looking and imagining if she would wear the same expression during sex or break that. Damn. Promise. "I love it out here. The mountains. The water. The quiet." She tilted her head. "What made you buy property here? I can see you in exotic, bustling, noisy cities, but this?" Once more she scanned the private beach that led down to the Sound and beyond that, the imposing and regal Mount Rainier as well as miles and miles of majestic trees. "I would never have pictured it."

He didn't immediately reply but, deeming it safe, studied her upturned face. Tight honey and cinnamon curls grazed her cheek and jaw. Unable to stop himself—and not wanting to—he clasped a spiral and wound his finger around it, tugging gently. He could so easily develop an obsession with the thick strands. Already imagined them billowing across his naked chest and abdomen, over his thighs. His grip tightened.

"Let's make a deal," he murmured. "I'll answer your question if you truthfully answer one of mine."

She scrutinized him, a tiny frown furrowing her brow, as

if trying to decipher the catch-22 in his proposal. Finally, she nodded. "Deal. You first."

Releasing the lock of hair, he shifted back a step and leaned an elbow on the railing. He parted his lips, but the words didn't rush to his tongue. These sharing-kumbaya moments didn't come to him easily... Correction, they didn't come at all. But the first rule of business was supply and demand. And if he wanted Sydney to give a piece of her truth to him, he would have to distribute a portion of himself, no matter how loudly and adamantly reason railed at him to keep his mouth shut. Knowledge was power, and people couldn't use it against him if he didn't offer it to them.

"When I was a kid growing up in Chicago, I dreamed of a place like this," he began quietly. "My uncle owned a small, cramped home on the South Side. He was proud of it—and he should've been. He'd bought it with his own hard-earned money, kept it ruthlessly clean, but in a bedroom the size of a closet, our house surrounded by run-down buildings and neighbors who were so close I could hear their thoughts..." He blew out a hard breath. "Sometimes it seemed as if I were suffocating. Drowning in people, noise." *Poverty.* "I always dreamed of mountains. This villa was one of the first homes I purchased when the company started making a substantial profit. I can"—he paused—"breathe here. It's wide-open, private. And it's where I come when I need to get away."

Tension strung him tight as he waited for her reaction. The picture he'd painted was a far cry from the life she'd enjoyed.

"I understand suffocating," she whispered. "I'm glad you have this." Wrapping both hands around her mug and holding it before her like a ceramic shield, she dipped her chin. "Okay. Go ahead and ask your question."

A corner of his mouth quirked. "You say that like you're about to face a firing squad. Mine is simple. Why have I never seen you wear your hair like this?" He tugged a long spiral once more.

Her gaze dropped to her cup as she dragged her fingers through the curls, self-consciousness in every movement. *Maybe not so simple after all.* "You've known me a handful of weeks."

"Okay," he conceded. "Do you wear it like this often?"

"No."

"Stop stalling. Why not?"

She heaved a sigh, tipped her chin up. "It's not a state secret or big deal. The straightened hair is more manageable and more appropriate for many of the events I attend. Less…wild."

"Bullshit."

"That seems to be your favorite word," she muttered around the rim of her coffee mug.

"One of them."

"Well, if it's such bullshit, why don't you tell me the truth?" she asked softy, but he would've had to be Helen Keller not to see the glint in her eyes or hear the anger in her murmur.

Edging closer and reclaiming the space he'd placed between them, he regarded her until a flush reddened her cheekbones and her sensual lips parted on a hitch of air.

"I think you're repeating what you've heard from your mother. Not appropriate. Wild. How about unseemly or common?" Something moved behind her unflinching gaze, and if he hadn't quoted Charlene Blake verbatim, then he'd struck close. He pinched a heavy lock between his fingers, rubbed the strands that resembled rough silk. "I understand certain fashions call for certain hairstyles. But the confined ponytails and buns? Those belong to Sydney Blake, the social princess, the beautification committee woman, the silent daughter of Jason Blake. But this?" He lifted the spiral, wove it around his finger. "This belongs to *you*. The Sydney who volunteers at the youth center. The Sydney who likes to sit on the back porch and stare at the water and distant mountains with a hot cup of coffee. The Sydney who has dreams she hides and believes no one notices. The Sydney who kisses like she invented sex and could make a man come just from having her taste in his mouth."

The gentle, hungry lap of water against the shore. The faint clatter of the chef finishing their dinner behind the glass doors. And the rough huffs of their breaths.

"I also know why you comply with those dictates, Sydney," he added, need like a serrated blade over his voice. "You don't want to be seen. You're comfortable fading into the background. But I have news for you, sweetheart. You can straighten your hair, wear the latest fashion trends that everyone else has on, sit in the farthest, darkest corner, and you would still be the center of attention. All eyes would still go to you when you enter a room."

"Lucas…"

"Luke," he corrected.

She frowned, thrown off guard. "What?"

"Luke. All my close friends—all being Aiden—call me Luke."

What was he doing? He didn't want her friendship or affection. The ship on respect had sailed the moment he'd threatened her father and blackmailed her. So what the hell was he doing? He didn't need to know her thoughts, past hurts, or dreams in order to screw her. But a woman like Sydney wouldn't give her body lightly. She would need an emotional connection to him in order to surrender everything. And he damn sure wanted—hungered for—everything. Him? It was purely physical. He didn't need to love or trust her to lose himself in her tight, hot core. And Sydney didn't expect either from him.

For the year they were together, they could enjoy a pleasant, sexually satisfying relationship. And at the end, walk away unscathed, intact.

A shutter seemed to slam shut over her face, blocking him from reading her thoughts. "But we're husband and wife, not friends," she reminded him, tone flat.

"One more bargain." He waited for her slight nod before continuing. "A truce. For the duration of this week. We have to live together as a couple for the next year. I'd rather the next three hundred and sixty-five days be harmonious instead of contentious. We can start here. This week. Try with me, Sydney," he murmured.

The ruthless businessman in him yearned to touch her, kiss her, force her agreement with desire. But not only did that damn promise stand in the way, but so did his very inconvenient conscience. He wanted her yes freely given.

Willingly given.

She studied him, her piercing inspection hovering between "I want to trust you" and "go to hell." After several long moments, a shaky breath escaped from between her lips, and the thick fringe of her lashes lowered.

"Fine. I'll try…Luke."

Chapter Fourteen

"I'm not putting that in my mouth."

"Sydney," Lucas began.

"No. Absolutely not."

He sighed. "You'll never know if you like it or not if you don't try it."

Sydney scrunched her face up. "I don't need to down a bottle of grease to know I won't like it or that it'll clog up my arteries. And eating that"—she pointed toward the aluminum-wrapped treat in his hand—"is the equivalent of drinking a lard cocktail."

He peeled back a silver flap and bit into the deep-fried Twinkie with a moan, his brilliant green-blue eyes fixed on her. She turned her head away, hiding the ripple of arousal in her belly at the low sound of pleasure.

"There should be a surgeon general warning slapped on that," she said.

"Come on, Sydney." He pinched off a piece of the

golden-brown cake and held it in front of her lips, a script flip of Eve offering Adam an apple. Except this apple had been submerged in grease and had a creamy filling. "One taste. You just might be surprised and love it."

Said in that wicked voice, he was temptation personified. And it would require a stronger woman than her to resist. Sighing and mentally handing over her I-am-woman-hear-me-roar card, she reached for the snack. But he shook his head and nudged her lips, his hooded gaze locked on her mouth. Obeying his silent demand, she opened and allowed him to place the treat on her tongue. The rough pad of his finger grazed her flesh as he withdrew, leaving his unique taste behind to mingle with the cake.

She stifled a shiver. Jesus. The man could transform breathing into foreplay.

A combination of crunchy batter, soft sponge cake, and thick cream melted on her tongue. She shivered again, but for a completely different reason. "So that's what a heart attack tastes like. I've always wondered." She sipped from her black coffee, trying to erase the overly sweet flavor from her palate. "In a word. Yech."

He chuckled and finished off the snack with relish. His obvious enjoyment was both baffling and sensual. She leaned on the railing and studied the gray-blue waters of Elliott Bay, hoping the busy and colorful tableau of Seattle's famous Pike Place Market would distract her from staring at Lucas as if his face contained the answers to the deepest mysteries of the universe. Like what happened to planes that entered the Bermuda Triangle? Or what really became of Amelia Earhart? And how many licks did it take to get to the center of a Tootsie Pop?

Lucas Oliver was another great mystery yet to be unraveled.

Over the last three days, he'd squired her around Bainbridge as well as escorted her to Seattle, a thirty-minute ferry ride across the Sound. They'd done simple things such as sailing, shopping, and in Seattle, visiting a museum, going to the movies. Then there'd been the touristy activities like riding to the top of the Space Needle and dining in the restaurant there, since she'd never been to the landmark, as well as strolling among the many shops and stalls that created the Pike Place Market. And when the sun sank for the day, they returned to the six-bedroom cabin for delicious dinners prepared by Lucas's personal chef. The past few evenings had been passed sipping coffee or wine in front of a fire or even in a fierce battle of Monopoly. Lovely. Unexpected. She could apply those terms to the past several days, but not relaxing. Too much vitality, energy, and sexuality hummed within Lucas for her to completely relax around him. But he still fascinated her. Enticed her to work loose the many layers that comprised the man who could be merciless one moment, seductive the next, and in another blink, quietly teasing.

She shifted her attention back to him and found his steady, unflinching gaze on her. Almost as if he'd been patiently waiting for her to look at him so he could capture her in his visual web.

"Even if I had photographic evidence that Lucas Oliver, CEO of Bay Bridge Industries, enjoyed eating deep-fried Twinkies, no one would ever believe me."

"Aiden would."

"Because he's your friend?"

"Because he used to go with me at least three times a week and buy them from the mall's food court."

Surprise pulsed inside her. "I didn't realize you and Aiden went that far back."

He nodded. "We met in high school, and he's been my best friend ever since."

"I should've guessed your friendship was more than business related. He's the only person I've seen dare to poke the Bea—" *Oh, hell.*

His dark eyebrow arched. "The Beast?" His lips twitched. "It's okay, Sydney. I know what they call me."

"I'm sorry," she said. The cool wind off the water couldn't extinguish the heat firing her skin. "That was rude."

"It was the truth," he stated. "I prefer you risk violating the polite rules of society and be honest rather than politically correct."

Said no one to her ever. Shaking her head, she amended, "I meant to say he teases you where others vacillate between stuttering and bowing and scraping. He isn't…intimidated by you."

"You aren't, either."

Of course she was.

Did she fear he would abuse her? No. Only cowards hurt women, and Lucas was many things—ruthless, determined, unyielding, complicated, unnerving—but not a coward. She didn't fear *him* but what he made her feel. What he could turn her into.

A needy woman desperate for love and attention. His love and attention.

A kernel of panic bloomed, as tiny and grating as a pebble in a shoe.

"Aiden and I have been through hell together," he continued. "I know his deepest fears and secrets, and he knows mine. That kind of loyalty and friendship isn't born in the boardroom." He paused. Studied her. "What has your father done to deserve that kind of loyalty from you?"

She jerked, taken aback by the sudden switch in topic. "What are you talking about? He's my father," she stammered.

"And he isn't the warmest, most affectionate or supportive man. He expected you to marry a man because it was a financial coup for him. Your happiness was incidental. What about him inspires such devotion from you?"

"It isn't what he's done, but what I did." The admission burst past her lips before she could contain it. Horrified, she pinched the bridge of her nose hard. Oh, God, why had she blurted that out? And especially with him? He wouldn't understand. Couldn't understand how guilt and shame could whittle a person down until nothing remained but slivers of who they used to be—or could've been. Not Lucas—

A big palm slid across her nape. Tugged her closer until her cheek pressed against a hard chest. "Go ahead." The order was a rumble beneath her ear, and a key that unlocked the story she'd never repeated to anyone.

"My brother, Jay, was the son my parents had been praying and waiting for, and they were so happy and proud. I was six when he was born, and though I loved him, I also resented him for stealing the attention away that had been solely mine up until that point."

At first, the explanation stumbled past her lips. But as they gained traction, the words rushed over her tongue, as if anxious to escape. In an instant, she was transported to that hot summer afternoon fifteen years ago.

"The summer I was ten, Dad often traveled, and in those days, Mom sometimes went with him. This particular day, they were both away, and since I couldn't go to my friend's house, I asked the nanny if I could go swimming. She'd said no, because Jay, who adored the water, had a cold and couldn't go with me. Mad, I waited until she became busy with Jay before pulling on my swimsuit—a black-and-white suit with pink ruffles around the leg. I'll never forget it," she whispered. Inhaling, she halted in the telling, the fierce pounding of her heart like an anvil against her sternum.

"I snuck out the back French doors and headed for the pool. Just as I went in, I realized I'd forgotten a towel and rushed back inside and up to my bathroom. Then I remembered I didn't have goggles, either, so I stopped to search for those, too. About ten minutes later, with my goggles and towel under my arm, I headed back to the pool. That's when I heard it. The scream. I'll never forget it," she breathed. Even now, all these years later, she could hear it, the terror and pain branded into her sensory memory. "I ran down the stairs, toward the rear of the house. Through the French doors I'd left open, I saw the nanny kneeling beside the pool, Jay's still body beside her. My parents were devastated. They returned home minutes after the ambulance arrived. I can remember Mother falling to her knees screaming, and Dad cradling his body, roaring. He looked at me and yelled, 'Your fault'…"

Her voice faded along with the bustling noise in the marketplace. The only sound she heard was the steady beat of Lucas's heart beneath her ear. His hand eased up her neck, burrowed through her hair, and cradled her head. The other palm stroked a path up and down her spine, his touch soothing, anchoring her in the present.

"You've blamed yourself for a mistake all these years? Tragic and horrible, God, yes. But still a mistake. For God's sake, Sydney..." His grip tightened in her hair, and he drew her head back to meet his gaze, bright with sympathy and anger. "You were ten. Who in the hell would blame a child?" When she didn't reply, he swore under his breath. "That's fucking crazy."

"He apologized later. Both he and Mom were devastated, in shock, and grieving. I understood. Still..." She studied the grim line of his mouth, his strong chin. "I've learned the brutal lesson of placing myself and my desires above others. My mistake cost them their son. And no sacrifice is too big, not when it will never restore what they lost." Conforming to their wishes, marrying a man they approved of but whom she didn't love, submitting to blackmail to save her father's company—none of those sacrifices seemed too big.

"Listen to me, Sydney," he growled, giving her head a small shake. "No one is to blame. Not you, who was being an average ten-year-old kid. Not the nanny, who mistakenly let your brother get away from her. Not your parents, who weren't home. Not your brother, who ran away and jumped into the pool. Sweetheart," he murmured, caressing her back one last time before cupping her jaw. "His death is not your burden. It's a tragedy, not a weight you're responsible for bearing." He hesitated, and a muscle in his lean cheek jumped. "And your father has sins he has to answer for, but not loving you isn't one of them." He ground out the admission as if it pained him to grant her father any concession. "He loves you. The day we married, he pulled me into my study to warn me not to hurt you. While I can't excuse him for blaming you, even as a knee-jerk reaction to his pain, he knows you've suffered, and he said you didn't deserve to endure any more pain. It might be the one thing he and I agree on. Let it go, sweetheart."

Knows you've suffered…didn't deserve any more pain… he loves you… The information whirled in her head like a mini twister, the revelations like madly dancing leaves she tried hard to grasp but couldn't.

"You said he has sins to answer for. Meaning what you believe he's done to you," she said. "But you've never told me what that is. Will you tell me now?"

Tension invaded his body. Though his touch remained gentle as he dropped his hand from her face and untangled his fingers from her hair, a wall of ice had dropped over his eyes. For the first time since they'd arrived in Washington, the pitiless, enigmatic mogul returned, the cold in his taut features and implacable gaze freezing her from the inside out.

"Are you ready?" He nodded toward her cup of coffee.

"Yes," she said, the lukewarm contents no longer comforting or appetizing. Silently, they headed toward the market's exit.

Though his abrupt withdrawal stung, and he remained as secretive as ever, one thing loomed crystal clear.

Whatever offense her father had committed, Lucas had appointed himself judge and jury. An unsettling thought wormed its way into her mind, and she couldn't rid herself of the taint. Unease twisted in her stomach, pushing the coffee she'd drunk toward her throat.

While trying to save her father, had she unwittingly contributed to his execution?

Chapter Fifteen

Lucas stared at the closed door of Sydney's room, his hand hovering above the knob. At the last moment, he rapped his fist against the door and waited. It'd been several hours since they'd returned to the house from the Pike Place Market and, claiming tiredness, she had closed herself in her bedroom.

Common sense had argued for granting her space and respecting her privacy. After the emotional outpour about losing her brother and the battle of guilt she'd waged all these years, she deserved some alone time to decompress. But the primal, possessive side of him snarled and snapped, demanded he push until she lowered both her emotional and physical barriers. It was hypocritical to want that from her when he wouldn't—couldn't—offer her the same. But the need that plagued him day and night didn't give a damn.

He'd capitulated to his common sense, but it'd been touch and go for a minute there.

But after hours without her company when he'd so easily become accustomed to her warmth and quiet wit, he was headed into withdrawal. And if it unnerved him how quickly he'd adapted to her presence, he didn't dissect it. Later. He'd conduct the analysis and study the results later.

The door swung open, and instantly, the persistent gnawing eased. Reserve and an aloofness smoothed Sydney's features into the beautiful, distant mask he detested. But this time, it didn't put him off. After the patience he'd exerted this afternoon, the cold, distant reception goaded him, challenged him. The hunger he'd throttled and reined in for the sake of his promise yanked at its leash, breaking it with an audible snap that reverberated inside his head.

Lunging, he thrust his fingers into her curls, snagged them in his fist, and pulled her head back. Her eyes widened, her hand slapping against his chest. Her lips parted, but he crushed his mouth to hers, swallowing her gasp. Her taste exploded across his tongue, and he groaned, diving deeper, taking more. After the smallest delay, she met him, greedy stroke for greedy stroke. Her palm slid up his chest, and both arms looped around his neck, holding onto him. Perched on her tiptoes, she opened wider for him, allowing him to claim more even as she conducted her own sensual advance, sucking on his tongue, licking the roof of his mouth. His grip on her tightened. The fingers in her hair angling her head for a deeper penetration. The hand on her hip steadying her as he ground his throbbing cock against the softness of her stomach. All afternoon, this gaping pit had yawned wide in his gut, and now with her tongue dancing with his, her curves pressed to him, desire rushed in, a roaring flood filling the aching emptiness.

Deliberately, slowly, he moved forward, guiding her

backward, never lifting his mouth from hers. When the backs of her knees hit the edge of the mattress, and she sank to the bed, he followed her down. Settling between her spread thighs, covering her. The softness of her breasts pillowed beneath his chest, the firmness of her thighs cradling his hips, the heat of her pussy that burned his cock even though her black lounging pants and his jeans... *Damn it.*

He slammed his palms to the bed on either side of her head and surged off her.

"I didn't come up here for this," he growled. "Dinner is ready, and I picked up *Grease* for you. I promised to give you time, and I'll keep it. So if you want to walk away from this, now is the time to do it. Because if you don't, I'm not stopping until I'm buried deep inside you."

Her lashes lifted, and his heart fucking stopped as her hands flattened over his shoulders. And pushed.

The bottom plummeted out of his gut, and he rolled over on his back, his arm thrown across his eyes. Damn. *Damn, damn, damn.* Air sawed out of his lungs, and his erection, rock hard and aching, pounded in time with his heart.

A few minutes. I just need a few minutes. Then maybe I can walk...

The room plunged into darkness, the pale moonlight streaming through the floor-to-ceiling windows providing illumination. He straightened, and if he hadn't been sitting, shock would've knocked him on his ass. Like a wet dream come to vivid life, she stood next to the bedroom door and the light switch she'd just flicked off...the sweater she'd just drawn up and over her head on the floor at her feet.

Shadows draped her, but they couldn't conceal the bared golden skin, the beautiful breasts cradled by black lace, the perfect indent of her waist and sexy flare of her hips. Neither could the darkness eclipse the courageous tilt of her chin or the instinctive tensing of her arms, as if she wanted to fold them around her torso, hide from him, but stopped herself.

Good. She was gorgeous. A voluptuous goddess in lace, silk, and knit instead of sea foam and shell.

Her thumbs hooked into the waistband of her pants. "Stop," he rasped. Cupping his hand, he beckoned her forward. "Come here." His voice, harshened by lust, sounded like sandpaper in the silent room.

Fierce satisfaction burned in him when she obeyed without hesitation. She retraced her steps to him, her feet soundless on the hardwood floor. When she stood between his thighs, he pulled her in those last few inches until the outside of her legs stamped the inside of his. Pressing his face to the smooth, flat expense of her abdomen, he breathed her in. Her sweet scent filled his nostrils, and he couldn't resist opening his mouth over her skin, sucking and licking as if he could draw the honey and cinnamon color onto his tongue.

Her soft sigh roughened as he moved up her torso to the shadowed valley between her breasts. He lingered there, lapping at the silken flesh not covered by black lace. Trembling beneath his hands, she threaded her fingers through his hair, clutching him close. He received her telegraphed message: more. Images of the night on the stairs after the gala, her breasts bared to him and his touch, infiltrated his mind. Hell, yes, he wanted that. More. He wanted his mouth to explore what his hands had already navigated. But first…

"Kiss me." He didn't wait for her to comply but grasped the back of her neck and drew her down. Gold and brown spirals surrounded his face, brushed his checks, jaw, and neck. Enclosing them in a sensual world of taste, sighs, and lust. Groaning, he parted her full lips with his tongue, and she yielded to him. He couldn't get enough of her mouth; he hadn't lied when he'd told her how he adored it. Fucking fantasized about it. He swept inside, thrusting, daring—demanding—and she partnered him in the erotic dance.

With her flavor sharp on his palate, he reluctantly abandoned the kiss to trail down her chin, across her jaw, and down the slender column of her neck. Damn, he wanted to linger, to savor. But he was also impatient as hell. Hunger and need rode him hard, relentlessly. The control it required not to rip the remaining clothing from her body and plunge between her thighs, first with his mouth, then his cock... He deserved a gold medal.

Leaning back, he rested a fingertip on her bra's front clasp. Lifted his gaze to hers. And waited. Only when she gave a tiny nod did he pop the closure and almost reverently peel back the cups. Sliding his fingers under the straps, he pushed the lace and satin down her arms.

"Beautiful," he murmured, drinking in the curves that pronounced—hell, shouted—she was a woman. "You're so damn beautiful." Full, satiny smooth and crowned by nipples of the richest caramel. "So damn sweet."

With a low rumble in his throat, he palmed her breasts, held one up to his lips, and sucked her into his mouth. Sydney cried out, jerked hard, but the grip on his hair tightened, grabbed him closer.

He coiled his tongue around the hard tip, licking it, savoring it. Worshipping it. She deserved to be worshipped, to be told even without words how gorgeous and sexy she was. Releasing her nipple, he switched to the other, lavishing the same attention on the peak while dragging his thumb back and forth across the wet, swollen nub he'd just enjoyed.

Small whimpers escaped her as she arched her back, offering him more of herself. Her hips rolled, wildly undulating, pleading. His cock pounded at the erotic sight of her hunger. Deftly, he switched their positions, flipping her onto the bed and her back. Quickly divesting her of her remaining clothing, he tossed the pants and matching black panties to the floor.

Desire pummeled the breath from his lungs. Slender shoulders, perfect breasts, and a small waist tapered into hips perfect for a man to dig his fingers into as he fucked with wild abandon. Toned, firm legs made for clasping a man's waist or shoulders. And his. For at least a year, she was his to touch, stroke, pleasure.

Whipping his sweater over his head, he placed a knee on the mattress. He palmed her thighs, spread them farther apart. And farther still. Wide enough to accommodate his shoulders. Curls denser and darker than the spirals on her head shielded her sex from him. But as he slid his hands under her ass and lifted her to him, nothing could hide the plump, feminine core of her or the glossy evidence of her desire from him. This close, he could smell the sweet and spicy perfume of her flesh. He'd been right. The honeysuckle scent was thickest here. His mouth watered for a taste, even knowing a sampling wouldn't satisfy the hunger burning a hole in his gut.

"Lucas," she gasped, her fingers scrabbling at his shoulders.

"Luke," he corrected, laying a kiss to the sensitive place where her thigh and torso connected. "In here, it's Luke." Why he pressed her on the less tangible but intimate connection of his shortened name, he couldn't explain. He just knew he wanted—needed—to hear it on her lips. Right here when they were about to become as close as two people could be. "Say it, Sydney."

A small hesitation, then, "Luke." She clutched his head, her fingertips a blunt pressure against his scalp. "Please," she breathed.

She didn't have to plead with him to take what he desired to claim. With a growl, he dipped his head and licked a path from the small, clenching entrance to the nub at the top of her glistening folds. Gently, he circled his tongue around her clit, lapping at the tight, pulsing kernel of flesh. But soon, it wasn't enough. Burrowing lower, he feasted. Sucked. Stroked. And thrust. Not one part of her remained a mystery to him. Even as her pleas and cries filled the room, he didn't stop. Not until he drew on her clit, plunged two fingers deep into her core, and the lush, muscled walls convulsed around him. Sydney thrashed on the bed, writhing, arching under his hand and mouth. Coming apart in a tableau so erotic, so hot, so feminine, he almost exploded with her.

When the last contraction ebbed, he gritted his teeth and slid his fingers from her slick heat. He lurched to his feet, snatched his wallet from his back pocket, and removed a foil packet. Tossing the billfold to the bedside table, he rid himself of his jeans. Just the economical strokes of his hand to sheath himself in the latex shoved his control closer and closer to no man's land. Stalking to the bed, he kneeled between her wide-spread thighs again, cupping the soft underside of them and pushing her legs back. Exposing her pink, swollen flesh to his ravenous gaze and his dick.

"Once isn't going to be enough, sweetheart," he warned

her, nudging the tiny entrance to the heart of her with the round head of his cock. "Once I'm inside your"—he pushed, and indescribable pleasure nailed him in the base of the spine, squeezed his balls—"pussy, once is not going to be nearly enough," he ground out. He withdrew, surged forward until half of the thick stem was submerged in her perfect, too-small core. "You're so tight. So wet. And it's for me."

Staring at the place where she flowered around him, he drew back once more, then with an animal-like grunt, thrust. Ecstasy ripped the shout from his throat, mingling with her throaty scream. All of him. She squeezed and rippled around all of him. *Damn*. He held himself brutally still. Sweat slid down his temple, dotted his shoulders and chest. Every muscle in his body strained, railed at him to take, to plunge, to fuck. A couple more minutes. Just a couple more, and he could scrape enough control together…

Then she reared up, wrapped her arms around his neck. And bit him.

The tattered leash on his restraint snapped.

Palms slamming down on either side of her head, he claimed her mouth in a voracious kiss as he dragged his cock from her flesh until her folds kissed the head. Then drove back inside. Her sex sucked at him like a mouth, caressing him, clasping him. He gripped her knee, hiked it higher around his waist, opening her more. Allowing him deeper.

He rode her like a man possessed, chasing pleasure like Ahab after his white whale. Their wet skin smacking together, their harsh breaths and her soft whimpers punching the air. Harder. Faster. Deeper. Harder. Faster. Deeper. Harder…

She screamed, tensed. And came. Her walls clamped down on him, milking him. He swallowed the sounds of her rapture and stroked through it, maximizing and stretching the orgasm out until she wilted beneath him.

Only then did he follow her into oblivion.

• • •

"Where are you going?"

Sydney paused in the middle of tying the sash of her robe at the slightly slurred question. She glanced over her shoulder at the rumpled blankets and sheets and the sexy-as-sin man in the middle of them. His hooded gaze swept over her no doubt mess of curls and down her body, now covered from neck to mid-thigh by her robe. When that stare, heavy lidded from drowsiness and sex, met hers again, unbidden pleasure unfurled inside her chest and belly, spreading to all points north and south. Especially south. *Good God.* He'd just subjected her to the most cataclysmic, earth-shattering orgasm of her entire life, and already her body craved more.

Dark waves falling around his face, he arched an eyebrow.

Right. He'd asked her a question. "For a drink of water. Are you thirsty?"

"No, but if you are, I'll get it." He threw the blankets aside and climbed from the bed. Within seconds, he had his jeans pulled over his lean hips, zipped but unbuttoned and leaving a tantalizing amount of skin exposed. Including the sensual vee of his hips that begged her tongue to trace.

Oh, God. Get a grip. Now.

"You don't have to—"

He gripped the nape of her neck and tugged her close for a quick, blistering kiss. "Yes, I do." He exited the room before she could mount an objection.

Several moments passed before she crossed the several steps that brought her to the bed and sank down to the mattress. Studying the dark blue sheets, she smoothed her fingertips across the soft material. Casting a quick glance at the partially closed door, she listened for the heavy fall of footsteps. Detecting nothing but quiet, she lifted the sheet to her nose and inhaled. Him. Her. Them. Sex. Pleasure. Pictures like a movie reel flashed on the back of her eyelids. His mouth on her breast. Between her thighs. The sharp angles of his face honed by lust as he rose over her, stroking inside her with a power and skill that stole her breath even now.

Heart pounding, she released the sheet. The floor would have to crack open and swallow her whole if he reentered the room to find her sniffing the blue cotton.

What did he think of her? Of her easy capitulation when she'd demanded time? Hell, what did she think of herself? The conversation on the boardwalk had planted a seed in her heart that she couldn't root out. A suspicion that the resentment and hatred Lucas harbored for her father hadn't been satisfied with their marriage. He was keeping secrets—secrets she feared would render her sacrifice null and void.

Yet when he'd shown up at her bedroom door, she'd surrendered to the need he'd instilled in her and nurtured with each touch, glance, and word. As soon as his mouth had covered hers, she'd been lost. And her submission had nothing to do with her father, contracts, or promises, and everything to do with pleasure and ecstasy only he could satisfy since only he had kindled it.

"What are you thinking about so hard?"

She started, pressing a hand to her chest. Either his predatory features extended to his movements or she'd been so deep in thought she hadn't even noticed his return. She scanned his flat, unreadable expression. Probably a little of both.

"Nothing, really."

"Ah." He settled the tray loaded with a pitcher of ice water, cold slices of chicken, cheese cubes, grapes, and a medium-sized loaf of baked bread on the bed. "A woman's 'nothing' is vastly different from a man's. Which means it could be anything from the state of the union to how I royally screwed up." He poured two glasses of water and placed them and the pitcher on the bedside table.

She scowled at him even as her stomach rumbled at the sight of the impromptu dinner. "That's not sexist at all."

He didn't reply but ripped off a corner of the loaf, placed cheese and meat on the bread, and passed it to her. Her heart tripped over itself at the seemingly unconscious kindness. As she accepted the makeshift sandwich, he closed his fingers over hers.

"Regrets already, Sydney?" he asked, the question a low ripple in the silent room.

"No." Once more she studied him. The piercing green-blue eyes that had blazed with scorching heat less than an hour ago but were now shuddered, impassive. The almost lush, sensual curve of his mouth that contrasted with the sharply hewn planes of his face. The hard, strong line of his jaw. The harsh imperfection of the scar that was perfect on him.

Confusion commingled, mated with the blush of arousal. Questions and concerns—she had dozens of those. But regret? No.

"Does it bother you?" He plucked up a slice of chicken and popped it into his mouth. God, it wasn't fair that he made eating with his fingers sexy, too.

She blinked, refocusing on their conversation. But couldn't follow. He'd lost her.

She frowned. "That we had sex?"

"No. The scar. You were staring at it. Does it bother you?" No emotion or inflection in the question, just a flat monotone that he could've used to ask the time of day.

Like the first time he'd asked that question three weeks ago—God, had it only been three weeks since he'd exploded into her life?—the quick "Not at all" rose to her tongue, hovered there. But at the last instant, she didn't utter the three words. Because they would be a lie.

"Yes," she murmured. Something flared in his gaze— something old and dark before it became as opaque as before. "But not for the reasons you probably think." She turned more fully toward him, tucking her foot under her thigh. "When I first met you, of course I noticed the scar. But I wasn't repulsed. I ached for you. For the pain you must've endured. It bothered me that you suffered." A scowl started to crease his brow, and she shot up her hand, palm out. "I don't pity you. No one who looks at you could ever feel sorry for you. You're too…dangerous for that." She huffed out a short bark of laughter. "I remember thinking you resembled a panther. Dark. Stunning. But predatory. The mark isn't a sign of your weakness but your strength. Your power to fight and survive. I find it…" She paused, weighed the judgment of revealing this particular truth.

He watched her like the animal she'd mentioned, his scrutiny steady, unblinking, as if searching her for any hint of a lie. Sighing, she rose from the bed, careful not to jostle the tray. She approached him, moved between his legs, and cupped his face.

"I find it beautiful," she whispered. Then laid a gentle kiss to the ridged flesh beneath his right eye before placing another on the twin scar that bisected his eyebrow. "I find you beautiful," she confessed against his skin.

His hands clutched her waist. Other than the tiny flexing of his fingers, he remained as still as a statue. No, that wasn't true. His eyes blazed with a fire that burned her.

Suddenly, he launched to his feet. In one explosive motion, he had her in the air, her legs wrapped around his waist. He strode across the room, and the moment her back touched the wall, he consumed her. His tongue dived between her lips, taking, conquering. The kiss was hard, explicit, primal. A clash of mouths, tongues, and teeth. She'd unleashed something wild in him, and it claimed her, branded her. Excitement and desire pumped through her veins, drenching the tender folds between her thighs. His chest pinning her, his hands forged a rough path down her sides and down to her thighs. He scraped her robe high, above her waist, before dropping his hand between her legs and shoving his pants down far enough to free his erection.

"Do I need a condom?" he growled against her mouth, the wide, flared head nudging her folds.

She clutched at his shoulders, tried to impale herself on his thick flesh. "I'm on the Pill," she rasped. "Unless you…"

"I'm clean. I've never fucked without protection. But you…" He flexed his hips, thrust inside her and groaned, the hoarse sound one of pained pleasure. "You, I want to feel naked, bare against my dick. Squeezing me, drenching me in all this wet heat. I want *you*."

And he took her.

Chapter Sixteen

"Congratulations," Aiden announced as he strode into Lucas's office, a sheaf of papers in his hand. He handed the stack to Lucas then dropped into the visitor's chair in front of his desk, long legs sprawled wide. "You now own 46 percent of the Blake Corporation." He paused. "And majority ownership."

Lucas examined the purchase agreement for twenty thousand shares of Blake Corporation stock in the name of one of his insurance conglomerates. With this latest acquisition, he owned almost half of Jason's company. Cold pleasure filled him, and he savored its icy embrace.

So close. He was so close to fulfilling the promise—ruining Jason Blake—he'd vowed over his father's grave so many years ago.

"No red flags?" Lucas glanced up from the contract.

"None. With you buying relatively small amounts through different corporations over the last couple of years, no one has caught on. As far as Jason Blake is concerned, he still retains the controlling shares in the company."

And he had. Jason possessed 44 percent of Blake Corporation's shares, the remaining split up between many stockholders. If any of the stock had been steadily scooped up by one entity, the company would have been put on alert that someone was attempting a possible takeover. But for two years, Lucas had been quietly purchasing stock as it became available through the many firms and businesses under the Bay Bridge Industries umbrella. As of today, he effectively owned controlling interest in Jason Blake's company.

Fruition of his revenge dangled like an apple on a just-out-of-reach branch. His fingertips grazed the prize, but couldn't grab it. Yet.

There remained one final step before he could claim victory. The step he relished above all the others.

"Have legal draw up a contract demanding Jason Blake resign as CEO and chairman of the board of directors of Blake Corporation."

Even as he uttered the request, an unbidden image of Sydney appeared in his head. Her, standing at the railing of the Seattle home, glancing over her shoulder and gifting him with one of her rare, unguarded smiles.

"Have you told Sydney about your past with her father?"

Sometimes Lucas swore the other man was a mind reader. And those times—like now—were damn annoying.

"No." Lucas tossed the contract on his desk. "I haven't."

Aiden scowled. "Why the hell not? So I guess you also haven't informed her of your plan to buy out her father's company from under him?"

"And risk her telling Jason? No. She has no loyalty

toward me."

"She might if you told her the truth. If you told her about why you've set this whole Machiavellian scheme in motion. But if you don't at least give her the benefit of the doubt, you're going to lose her."

"Lose her?" Lucas scoffed, falling back in his chair. "You say that like I ever had her."

The truce he and Sydney had agreed on in Seattle had remained intact since their return to Boston three weeks earlier. Their lives had fallen into an alarmingly domesticated pattern: he left early in the morning for the office, and she spent most of her day at the youth center. She arrived home before he did and arranged for dinner to be ready when he walked through the door. They dined together, discussing neutral topics such as her work at the center and invitations she'd accepted on their behalf. Afterward, he'd disappear inside his study to finish up anything he hadn't been able to address during the day. And then...then he entered their room, where he and his wife had sex until neither one of them could move. At the bedroom door, all polite civility ended, and they took each other with a wild abandon that pleased and shocked the hell out of him.

And left him hungry.

Not just for her body and all that startling, amazing passion, but for *her*. The parts of herself she doled out to Yolanda and Melinda Evans and the girls at the youth center, but not to him. Unless she was writhing under him in bed, losing control. Only then did she lower her guard. He'd believed he would be satisfied with sex—didn't want any more than that. He'd been wrong.

Especially when Tyler had possessed more of her than

Lucas had. Her ex-fiancé had earned her friendship, her esteem, her affection. Hell, on their wedding night, she'd asked for more time because of Tyler. Lucas clenched his fist, hating the dual serrated edges of helplessness and jealousy sinking their jagged teeth into his chest.

"The world is not some fairy tale, Aiden. You and I know that better than anyone. Sydney married me because I blackmailed her. She wanted to save her father from jail, and I wanted to prevent Jason from getting his hands on Tyler Reinhold's money." If he hadn't interceded, she would be planning her engagement party to another man at this moment.

"Yet you're the only one winning in this situation. Jason may not go to jail, but you're going to ruin him. And you used his daughter to do it. Have you even considered how that's going to devastate her?" Aiden snapped.

"What do you want me to do?" Lucas shot from his chair, as if trying to escape the guilt that slicked his skin, invaded his pores. He stalked to the large window overlooking the financial district as well as the west entrance to the Public Garden. If he squinted, he could make out the statue of George Washington on horseback. Normally, he enjoyed the view. But at this moment, he hardly noticed it. "Turn my back on the promise I made to my father? Just let Jason Blake get away with the damage he's done? Because of him, I grew up without a father. He laid waste to my life."

"No, he didn't," Aiden murmured. "Luke, you are a successful, respected businessman who owns and runs one of the largest conglomerate organizations in the world. You've achieved the impossible from most people's viewpoint—emerging from the inner city of Chicago's South Side to beat the odds as a powerful, wealthy man." He sighed, pushing himself out of his chair. "I'm your friend, so when I say this, I'm leaning on that friendship. It isn't Jason Blake's fault you grew up without a father… It's your father's fault."

Lucas remained still, but inside, he flinched as if Aiden had sucker punched him in the chest. "Everything I've done, everything I am is because I swore one day he would pay for all the pain and loss he's wreaked. And you want me to choose between my father and a woman I met less than two months ago? A woman who's made it clear her first loyalty is to the man who stole the one person I loved most and my childhood from me?"

"No," Aiden said quietly. "I want you to choose between living and existing."

· · ·

"Thank you, James." Sydney smiled at Lucas's driver as he clasped her hand and guided her from the backseat of the luxury town car. "I should be ready about one thirty. If I'm running later than that, I'll call you."

He dipped his head in acknowledgment. "I'll wait here for you, Mrs. Oliver."

Mrs. Oliver. One month, and she still hadn't become used to the new last name. Or the enigma that was her husband. After the week in Seattle, she'd believed they had at least established a basis for friendship. But after they'd returned home, Lucas had become remote—more so than before their honeymoon.

Except at night.

At night he changed into the fierce, passionate lover

who'd introduced her to a pleasure beyond her wildest imagination. As if the moon spilling across the hardwood floors of their bedroom transformed the cold, reserved man into a voracious beast.

Putting those thoughts out of my head right now.

God, if she walked into this restaurant for lunch with her mother flushed and aroused, Charlene wouldn't stop pestering her until she ferreted the truth out of Sydney. And as nosy as her mother could be, she doubted Charlene would appreciate all the salacious details of her daughter's love life.

And they were salacious.

Smoothing a palm down the side of her black pencil skirt, Sydney double-checked the white peasant-style shirt for wrinkles and the stiletto boots for scuff marks. Her mother's vision could shame an eagle into visiting an optometrist; she wouldn't miss the slightest imperfection.

Inhaling, she entered the upscale restaurant at which Charlene had called and requested Sydney meet her for lunch. Threading through the semi-crowded dining area, she spotted her mother at a table near the wide front window.

Charlene rose and lightly kissed her on either cheek. The familiar scent of Chanel No. 5 enveloped Sydney, and a rush of emotion poured through her—joy at seeing her mother after weeks of no contact, sorrow at the estrangement, apprehension over the confrontation. Because with her mother, there was no such thing as a simple lunch.

"What did you do to your hair?" Charlene grimaced, pinching a curl. "God, Sydney, you look like a ragamuffin. Does Lucas Oliver not allow you to visit a stylist or at least buy you a dryer?"

The criticism stung, but Sydney covered it with a

courteous smile as she lowered to the chair across from Charlene and fought the habitual urge to apologize. Not only did Lucas seem to like the full tumble of spirals, but she'd grown to love the natural style. At what point did she stop allowing her mother to make her feel like a five-year-old instead of a twenty-five-year-old capable of making her own decisions? Of feeling unworthy?

"You're looking beautiful, Mom." She picked up the linen napkin and flicked it open to settle over her lap. "How's Dad?"

"Thank you. And he's fine. Worried, but fine." Her mother picked up her glass of white wine and sipped, studying her over the rim. "I'm surprised by your concern. It's been four weeks since your"—pause—"wedding. And we haven't heard from you once."

Charlene was not just her mother, but the mother of guilt trips, also. "After our last conversation, I assumed we both needed time." Their waiter appeared, setting a plate of hot, fresh bread on the table. Sydney placed her order for a shrimp salad before returning to her mother and plucking up a slice of the honey oat loaf.

Charlene's mouth scrunched into a moue of distaste. "Really, Sydney. Bread? As if you need any more carbs." She sighed. "I don't know how many times I've warned you to be careful of what you eat. Women of your"—another significant pause—"stature have to be more vigilant and careful than others."

Sydney set the slice on her plate and folded her hands in her lap. "Stop it, Mom," she said softly, though she instilled a vein of steel in the order that halted Charlene mid-diatribe. "I'm not going to let you talk to me like that any longer."

Charlene huffed out an impatient breath. "The dramatics, Sydney—"

"Through pointed reminders and criticisms, I have understood for a very long time that I am not a perfect size two. I also know that disappoints and embarrasses you."

In her head, Lucas's voice echoed, rebounding against the walls, and gaining volume with each pass.

"Have your parents ground you down to the point where you believe you deserve that kind of treatment…"

She could still feel Lucas's palm against her jaw. Still see the fire that had blazed in his turquoise gaze as he'd made her contemplate herself in front of that mirror.

This woman is the most conscientious, selfless, considerate person I've met. And I've known her for weeks. How do they not recognize it…why does she let them get away with not acknowledging it? With not respecting her gifts, her heart, her feelings?

"I love you, Mom," she continued, shaking off the memory. "But if my stature aggrieves you that much, we can limit our interaction. And when we are together, I'm no longer going to allow you to put me down for it."

Silence, heavy with tension, loomed over their table like a single gray storm cloud.

"Well," Charlene said, tone as stiff as her spine. "Apparently being married to Lucas Oliver has also taught you how to be disrespectful."

Sydney didn't reply. Anything she uttered now would be construed as an apology, and she was not sorry for finally— *finally*—standing up for herself. Fighting for herself. Elation, airy and bright as a summer ray of sunshine, glowed inside her chest. No doubt, her mother viewed this as an opening volley in a bid for control, but damn it, for the first time she didn't fold, believing the outcome a foregone conclusion.

"Mrs. Williamson asked about you at our literacy meeting." Charlene took another sip of wine. "She wanted me to pass along her congratulations."

"Thank you. I'll have to call on her." Pleasantries. Trivialities. Safe topics.

"I told her you might." Then she launched into a detailed account of the events and parties she'd attended as well as the local gossip, not halting as the waiter returned and set their orders before them. "I accepted the invitation on your behalf to the Reinholds' reception after the *Carnaval* ballet opening this weekend. I'll send the car—"

"Wait, I'm sorry," Sydney interrupted, tuning back in. "Mom, why would you do that? I can't go to the Reinholds'."

"Of course you will," she dismissed with a careless flick of her hand. "I think it's very gracious of them to invite you after your treatment of Tyler. It would've been rude to decline."

"Yes, it is beyond generous of them to ask Lucas and me to their home, but I can imagine how awkward it would be."

"I didn't mention Lucas Oliver," Charlene corrected coldly. "The invitation was for you alone."

"And you agreed?" She gaped at her mother. "You expect me to attend the party hosted by my ex-fiancé and his family *without* my husband. That's ridiculous."

"You can go, Sydney. It's the least you can do for the Reinholds as well as for your father and me. They are extending the olive branch, and I must insist you accept it."

Anger at her mother's presumptuousness and cavalier rejection of Lucas sparked fast and hot. "Mom, I—"

"Excuse me. I hope I'm not intruding."

Oh, God. Sydney briefly closed her eyes. *Not now.* Why *now*?

"Tyler." Charlene rose, a beaming smile wiping away the chilly disapproval she'd worn seconds earlier. Her mother clasped Sydney's ex-fiancé's hands and pressed her cheek to his. "How wonderful to see you."

"And you're beautiful as always, Charlene." His gaze shifted to Sydney, who'd remained seated, shocked. A whisper of suspicion that this chance meeting wasn't so chance filtered through her brain. And a quick glance at her mother's smug smile confirmed it. "Sydney." He bent, lightly brushed his lips over her cheek.

A month ago, before the engagement had been broken off, the touch would have been nothing more than a polite greeting. But now she fought the impulse to recoil. Somehow, receiving a kiss from another man seemed…wrong.

"Hello, Tyler," she murmured. "I hope you've been well."

"Yes, as well as can be expected." The tone of his voice dropped, infusing the words with an intimacy that slithered over her skin. His gaze skimmed over her face, a heat she didn't remember ever glimpsing before lighting his gaze. Nervous nausea bubbled in her stomach. "I've missed you."

"Won't you join us?" Her mother gestured toward an empty chair as she reclaimed her own. "I was just telling Sydney about the invitation to your reception this weekend. Your mother was so kind to include us."

"I hope you'll come," he said, his intense perusal never leaving Sydney's face.

"I RSVP'd just this morning." Satisfaction practically purred in Charlene's tone.

"Wonderful," Tyler murmured. "I'm disappointed I can't stay for lunch. I have to return to the office for a meeting. But I'm thrilled I was able to see you before the reception. Now I have even more to look forward to."

Confused, Sydney stared after him as he rejoined his group and exited the restaurant.

"You arranged that *accidental* meeting." Sydney contemplated the pleased upturn of Charlene's lips. "Am I wrong?"

"Please," her mother scoffed. "You're so dramatic lately. I saw him at the Miltons' a couple of nights ago and mentioned we would be having lunch today. He seemed delighted to see you, though."

"I'm married, Mom," she stated.

Charlene waved off her words. "We both know that event shouldn't have happened and can easily be annulled. And when Tyler expressed how much he missed you the other night, I knew there was still a chance for this whole sordid mess to be over."

Sydney calmly set her napkin on the table beside her uneaten salad and rose from the table.

"Where are you going?" Charlene demanded. "You haven't touched your meal. And we still have details to discuss —"

"I'm leaving." Sydney slid her purse strap over her shoulder. "My appetite has suddenly vanished."

"Sit down," Charlene hissed, her gaze darting around the dining room. "I will not have you make a spectacle of us."

"I anticipated us having a nice, quiet lunch together, but you viewed it as an opportunity to ambush me. I won't have you disrespect me, Lucas, or my marriage by playing matchmaker." A tremor shook the last few words. She'd been surprised but happy that her mother had reached out to her. That she'd made an effort to bridge the gap between them. That she'd cared. *God, what a fool.* "I took vows, made promises. I won't betray them. Not for you, not for Dad, and certainly not because of a party invitation. Good-bye, Mom."

She didn't wait for her mother's response or castigation, because they would be one and the same. As she crossed the dining area and left the restaurant, fury and sorrow continued to burn inside her. Charlene wouldn't so easily forgive Sydney for walking out on her. But by her actions, her mother had jeopardized the agreement between Sydney and Lucas. And therefore risked her father's freedom.

And if a small, irritating voice pointed out that it'd been her mother's disdain of Lucas that had angered her, not the thought of the contract... Well, it was small enough to ignore.

Chapter Seventeen

Two o'clock in the afternoon. The CFO had called for a meeting to discuss the upcoming end-of-quarter, end-of-year budget. Aiden had scheduled a teleconference with potential buyers for the sale of one of their retail companies. And Lucas's assistant had forwarded him a list of calls that needed to be returned before the end of the day. He'd never neglected a meeting, a phone call, hell, an email in favor of a woman before.

Yet Lucas stood at the large bay window in his living room watching Sydney step out of the town car like some voyeur.

If he possessed even an ounce of common sense, he would return to the office, chalk this up to a moment of lunacy, and forget it happened…

He remained at the window.

Aiden's words haunted him as Sydney waved at James and climbed the front steps to the brownstone. "*She might if you told her the truth. If you told her about why you've set this whole Machiavellian scheme in motion. But if you don't at least give her the benefit of the doubt, you're going to lose her."*

He'd never had a woman who was solely his. His mother hadn't been his or his father's. She'd belonged to any man with a pretty face or deep enough pockets to keep her in the expensive clothes and jewels she adored. The women Lucas had been with had been expedient and expendable—by choice. Not until Sydney had he experienced this…this nagging persistence to possess, to smash down any wall she erected that kept him on the outside when he wanted in.

At the end of the year, he would walk away, but during the next eleven months…he wanted in.

"What are you doing home?"

Her surprised question brought him around, and the customary burn of desire flared to life. To not want her was like ordering his breath to freeze in his lungs. From the moment he'd bent over her hand at the auction and looked up into her lovely hazel eyes, lust for her had set up residence inside him and refused to be evicted.

"How did your lunch go?" he asked, sidestepping the question.

She sighed, untying the sash at her waist and removing her coat. As she crossed the room to toss the clothing over the back of the sofa, he dropped his attention to her ass in the slim-fitting black skirt. He bit back a groan. And made a mental note to buy one of those ass-hugging skirts in every color of the rainbow and in between.

"It was…interesting." She emitted another weary sigh and dragged a hand through her curls. "Between my mother calling me on the carpet for my hair, eating habits, and choice in husband, I ordered a salad I didn't get to eat. A salad that looked delicious, by the way."

Fury stirred in his gut, poked to flames by Sydney's abridged recounting of her conversation with her mother.

"Why didn't you get to eat it?" he asked, surprised by how calm he sounded.

"Because I walked out." She huffed out a strained chuckle. "I walked out," she repeated as if in disbelief. He took a step toward her, her name on his lips, but she shot up a hand, halting him. "No, I walked out," she said for the third time, stronger, firmer. "But not before telling her I would no longer put up with her criticism and digs at my expense. Granted, most of them are not malicious. But I think the indifference behind them is somehow worse. As if the in-ventorying of my imperfections is so common, so natural, it doesn't require spitefulness."

"Sweetheart," he murmured, eliminating the distance between them until her palm pressed into his chest.

"I love her," Sydney whispered, her fingers curling into his shirt. "For so many years, I tried to be perfect—the per-fect daughter, perfect hostess, perfect socialite—but I always failed. I just wanted them to love me, accept me, *for me*."

"Sydney." He brushed a knuckle down the golden soft-ness of her cheek. "They do. Maybe they're unable to show it, but they do." Part of him rebelled at the idea of defending her parents, but this wasn't about them; it was about Sydney. And to erase her pain, he would lie to Jesus Christ Himself.

"I was afraid," she admitted softly. "Does that make me a coward? At twenty-five years old, I was afraid to tell my own mother to back off."

"No, that doesn't make you a coward," he assured her, cupping her jaw and rubbing his thumb along the satiny skin.

"But," she continued as if he hadn't spoken, "I was more afraid to be silent. It's like something rose in me and warned me that if I didn't speak this time, I wouldn't do it again. That if not then, I would have been silenced for good. And that I couldn't bear."

Gently pushing her arm aside, he shifted, bringing them chest to chest, thigh to thigh. He cradled her face, grazed a kiss over her lips once. Twice. And once more. "I'm proud of you, sweetheart. What you did today…it took courage, not cowardice." He drew in a deep breath, stepped back, and dropped his arms to his sides. "Will you let me show you something?"

. . .

Sydney focused on Lucas's broad shoulders and how his thick, black waves brushed the collar of his shirt as she followed him through the house and down the stairs to the brownstone's garden level and into his study. Her lips tingled from his barely there kisses, the tender caresses so different from their usual raw, wild meeting of mouths. She lifted her fingers and pressed the tips to her skin. As he rounded his desk and glanced up at her, she dropped her hand as if caught doing something wrong—or incredibly telling.

He stared at her, that enigmatic gaze touching on her mouth before he beckoned her closer. Once she reached the massive pierce of furniture he worked at nightly, he opened a drawer and withdrew a manila folder. Without a word, he extended it toward her. Curious, she accepted and flipped it open. On top lay an old newspaper article, yellowed around the edges and wrinkled as if it'd been handled many times before. She scanned the headline: BOSTON-BASED FINANCIAL EMPIRE CLOSES ITS DOORS. BANKRUPT. The clipping, dated fifteen years earlier, contained a grainy picture of a building and a handsome man with dark hair and piercing eyes of an indeterminate color in the black-and-white image. Beneath it, the caption read, "Robert Ellison, CEO and co-owner of the Dighton Group." She frowned. The name seemed familiar, but it didn't ring any bells.

The article behind the first snatched the air from her lungs. An obituary. For a Jessica Ellison. Another picture. This time of a breathtaking woman whose features bore a hint of familiarity. Again dated fifteen years ago. No cause of death was listed.

And the last clipping, the blaring headline compounded the ache building behind her sternum. FORMER BOSTON EXEC COMMITS SUICIDE IN HIS HOME.

"Your father?" she rasped, her brain finally recognizing Robert Ellison. The man standing several feet in front of her shared the same sharp, angular bone structure. The mouth had been firmer, not as curved, and the black hair shorter, but the shape of his eyes, the arrogant slashes of eyebrows… those had been the same as Lucas's.

He nodded, the motion abrupt.

Lowering to the chair flanking his desk, she flipped back to the original newspaper article and began reading. Twenty minutes later, she'd read all three pieces and perused the other items in the file. Pictures of both the man and the woman—Robert and Jessica Ellison—with a small boy. More clippings about Jessica from society pages. A death certificate for Robert — GSW to the head. As an avid fan of *CSI* and *Grey's Anatomy*, she understood the term. Gunshot wound. Legal name change documentation for Brandon Ellison to Lucas Oliver.

Oh, God.

She lifted her head, met his implacable stare. None of what she'd read was common knowledge. After first meeting him, she'd scoured the internet for information about Lucas Oliver. And his father's identity and suicide, his mother, her death, his real name — *oh, God, his real name* — hadn't popped up in any of the results. What…? Why…?

"Why are you showing this to me?" she breathed, barely able to shove the question past her constricted vocal cords.

He smiled, the gesture humorless. "I was reminded earlier today of risks. And with your mother, you took the biggest of all. Rejection. If you can, then so can I." He dipped his head toward the folder. "That's me in all my ugly, naked truth. It's why I came to Boston. It's why I am."

Yet the articles were half the story. They told about his parents' tragedy and deaths. The photos captured moments forever frozen in time. The documentation revealed impersonal, recorded facts. But they didn't tell *his* story.

She set the folder on the top of the desk. "Tell me," she whispered.

He remained standing, propping a shoulder against the window frame, his bright eyes remote and diamond hard, his full lips firmed into a grim line. His big body resembled a statue, rigid and unmoving.

"My parents were never what you would call happily married. My father doted on my mother, loved her to distraction — maybe obsession. But she didn't love him the same way. He was older than her by over ten years, and soon she didn't want to stay at home with an old man, as I heard her put it many times during their arguments. She cheated—it was her favorite pastime besides shopping. And my father's was turning a blind eye to her blatant infidelities. Until there was one betrayal he couldn't ignore."

His posture and tone remained the same, but still she sensed a change in him. And she braced herself.

"I was fourteen. I had stayed home from school that day because of a cold. Tired of being cooped up in my room, I'd gone downstairs for a snack, and that's when I heard them in the study, arguing. Nothing new about that except it was one o'clock in the afternoon. Dad was never home from work that early. I remember stopping outside the cracked study doors, eavesdropping, my stomach hurting. But not from being sick. I knew something was different. My father never yelled, no matter how mad Mom made him. But this time, he was screaming at her. His business partner. His best friend. The man he'd trusted most. She'd slept with him. He was devastated. I'd never heard that agony in his voice before. And she…she didn't give a damn."

Lucas couldn't conceal the bitterness and rage. It spilled through, burning away the cold in his voice, though his face remained impassive. Her fingers itched to touch him, to try and soothe the hurt in the only way she knew how. The only way he would allow.

"From that day forward, everything spiraled down at lightning speed. Dad stopped going into the office, just shut himself up in the study. He couldn't face the man who'd betrayed him with the one person he'd loved most in the world. And his partner took full advantage of my father's grief. Not

three months after Dad found out about them, his friend" —
Lucas spat the word — "formed his own company, convinced
the bulk of their clients to follow him, and left my father
with a failing, bankrupt business. He was dealing with that
when Mom — " He broke off, straightened, and stalked to
the bar. Several long moments passed as he poured himself
a drink and threw it back, barely flinching. After he served
himself another one, holding the squat tumbler in his hand,
he continued. "Mom and I were in a car accident."

Sydney gasped, horror squeezing her heart in a pitiless
fist.

"Is that where you were…"

"Scarred? Yes. While she argued with her current lover
on the phone, the traffic light changed from yellow to red,
and she didn't notice. We were T-boned, and we spun out,
wrapped around a tree. She died instantly."

"Oh, Jesus, Luke," she whispered. "You were trapped in
the car with her."

Again, an abrupt dip of his head. "Mom was dead, I had
a broken arm and was permanently scarred, and the business my father had built was gone, stolen. I think Mom's
death was it for him. Though she'd betrayed him over and
over again, had eventually left him, he still loved her. One
day, about three months after the accident, he told me he
was sending me to Chicago for the summer. To get me out
of Boston and away from the memories. I didn't want to go,
but Dad was adamant. My flight was supposed to leave on a
Tuesday morning, but when the car arrived at the airport, I
lied and told the driver I'd forgotten my ticket. We returned
home, and I went directly to Dad's study, ready to argue with
him. But when I pushed the door open, I saw…"

He stopped, a muscle ticking alongside his jaw, his knuckles clenched so tight around the glass they blanched white. Unable to remain in her chair any longer, she rose and went to him. Pried the tumbler from his hand. Wrapped her arms around him. Squeezed him tight, as if she could transfer her warmth to him. As if she could absorb his pain. Several seconds passed. Then his arms encircled her.

"He must've done it as soon as I left. The smell, the blood…" He shuddered, the tremble quaking through her. "Afterward, I found out he'd made arrangements before… before. Living with my uncle, his half brother I'd never met or knew existed. The adoption. The name change. The note he left me said he wanted to give me a fresh start without the taint of his name and legacy. I would've gladly carried his name," he swore fiercely. "Proudly. But it had been his last wish, and I couldn't deny him that. But as I stood over his grave, I promised I would regain everything that had been stolen from him."

"Luke." She reached up, swept her thumbs over the lean lines of his cheeks, over the patrician bones. Over the tough skin of his scar. "He would be proud of you. You've achieved everything he had and more. That's what he wanted for you. But," she rasped, shaking her head, "you have to stop blaming yourself."

He stiffened against her. Grabbed her wrists as if to snatch her hands away from him. But she tightened her hold, gripping his scalp.

"That's bullshit," he growled. "I don't blame myself."

"Yes, you do. Do you think I can't recognize guilt when I see it? After it's been my best friend for so long? If you'd turned around ten minutes earlier, you could've stopped him. If you'd refused to go to Chicago instead of giving in, he would've delayed his plans and eventually changed his mind. Anything you did wouldn't have changed his mind. You said he already had arrangements in place. He was determined, and your love for him and his for you wasn't enough to keep him here."

The last sentence rang in the room. His turquoise gaze nearly singed her in its intensity, and she refused to back down from it.

"And it's okay to be mad at him for it, Luke. After our talk in Seattle, I returned to my room and admitted that all these years I had secretly been mad at my little brother for jumping in that pool. He'd known better. But it was okay for me to be angry with him, because I missed him. I loved him. Your father left you. He didn't stick it out for you. Being furious with him doesn't mean you love him any less."

His grip on her wrists tightened just shy of pain. Had she pushed too hard? Too soon?

"Luke, I—"

His mouth closed over hers, purloining whatever words would've come next. Along with her breath. The kiss…it was soft. Gentle. Almost reverent. No less breathtaking and powerful than his usual erotic conquering, but…different. She opened under him, submitting to his particular brand of passion as she usually did. But after a few moments, she pulled away, cupped his face, tilted it down. And took control.

She pressed her lips to his forehead, his eyes, the scar, each cheek, his chin. When he tried to recapture her mouth, she avoided him and continued her path over his jaw, down his strong throat and over the shallow dip in his collarbone revealed by the freed top button of his shirt. His scent and taste—fresh rain after a storm and warm skin—roused her desire from simmering coals to hot, licking flames.

With suddenly clumsy hands, she opened his shirt, the buttons seeming to shrink in size as she fumbled to release them. Finally, she slipped her hands underneath the gaping material and curved her palms over his shoulders. Sighing at the taut flesh over solid muscle, she slid his shirt from his shoulders. When they pooled at his wrists, he made quick work of removing the cuff links and stripping the clothing off.

Since they'd first made love in Seattle, she'd seen him naked many times. She wouldn't need sight to trace the delineated ridges of his abdomen, the silken trail of hair bisecting his stomach, or the corded muscle along his thigh. Still, that didn't keep her breath from snagging in her throat at his masculine beauty. Slowly, she stroked her palms over his broad shoulders, down his toned arms to tangle her fingers with his. Rising on tiptoes, she grazed a kiss over his pectoral muscles, down the strip of skin between before shifting to a small, flat nipple.

"This is for you," she murmured against his skin, flicking the tip of her tongue over the dark brown disc. "Let me return the pleasure you always give me."

Not waiting for his response, she sucked on the hard nub, lightly biting down and soothing the sting with her tongue. Above her he swore, the curse harsh, strained.

"Again," he ordered hoarsely. "Your teeth. Do it again."

She complied, grazing the edge of her teeth over the peak before capturing it and nipping. Then she switched to the other nipple, treating it to the same attention, swirling, teasing, worrying it. His low growl vibrated under her mouth, the rhythmic clenching on her fingers quickening, becoming more aggressive. She released his hands, and they automatically darted to her head, sinking into her hair, twisting, pulling, and the tiny stings to her scalp added to the heat pouring through her veins. Yes, she kissed and tormented him. But his grunts of pleasure, the coarse groans of "fuck yes" and "harder, sweetheart," and the tense pull of muscles were like sensual caresses stoking the fire in her higher, hotter.

With a murmur, she sank to her knees, her lips tracing the light trail of black hair that disappeared beneath the waistband of his slacks. Like his shirt, she attacked the closure, but unlike then, with surer fingers. She lowered the zipper's tab, and the metallic teeth opened with a muted hiss, revealing the band and front of his black boxer briefs. Dipping her hand inside, she fisted hot steel flesh that pulsed with its own heartbeat. Their moans of pleasure mingled as she freed the long, thick column of his cock.

"Sydney." More tingling to her scalp, his tugging more insistent, more demanding. "Sweetheart…"

She parted her lips over the smooth knob of the head and engulfed it, dancing her tongue under the pronounced ridge. His scent was concentrated here, stronger and fused with the musk of sex. She loved it. Loved this act of simultaneous dominance and submission. The giving and taking. Because while she wrapped her hand around the base of his erection, languorously pumped while ravenously sucking him deep, she also received pleasure. Loving him, making him tremble and strain under her hand and mouth was the sweetest and most potent aphrodisiac. She squeezed her thighs against the merciless spasming of her core, wanted to slide her fingers beneath her skirt and stroke her aching clit and drenched folds. But that would require letting go of his cock or his hip, and she wasn't willing to do that.

Hard but considerate hands held her still as he took her mouth, whispering encouragement and praise when she allowed him deeper. She held on, trusting him, needing to see him lose the control he wore like a second skin. But as his cock swelled and his thrusts shortened, Lucas swore, jerked from between her lips, and yanked her to her feet. And when he crushed her mouth to his, the gentleness of before had evaporated under lust and a voracious greed. He wrenched her shirt over her head, snatched down the cups of her bra, and feasted on her breasts. Ecstasy boomeranged from her nipples to her core and back again. She clutched his head to her as he alternated between tugging on the tips with his fingers and tongue and drawing them deep into his mouth. It was so much—too much. She needed…

Reaching behind her, she grabbed the tab of her skirt.

"No." His fingers closed around hers, removing them. "Leave it on. Boots, too."

He hauled the skirt up her legs until the black material pooled around her waist. Cool air brushed over her legs, her behind, and the damp flesh between her thighs. A wrench, and her ruined underwear floated to the floor, leaving her even more bared. And vulnerable. With her bra shoved under her breasts and her skirt bunched around her hips, she shivered, the state of half dress somehow more exposing than if she were fully naked.

"Luke." She reached for him, needing his fierce passion to sweep her away. Hands cupping her ass, he maneuvered her to the brown leather couch against the far wall. He lowered to the cushions, drawing her down with him so she straddled his lap. The soft material of his suit pants brushed her inner thighs, a sharp contrast to the aggressive thrust of his cock against her folds and clit. She gasped, rolled her hips, and whimpered at the pleasure that lanced her.

Once more taking control, she rose on her knees, fisted the wide base of his erection, and slowly slid down. The head parted her, paving the way for the thick, large column to follow. Oh, God, he filled her. Stretched her. Branded her. After so many times, she should be used to the first resistance of her body to his penetration, but how could a person become accustomed to pleasure so acute it treaded the delicious, startling line of pain and ecstasy?

Tiny, breathless cries escaped her throat as she rose and fell, rose and fell, swallowing more of him on each return until she surrounded every inch of him. Beneath her, he strained, a fine tremble quivering through his big body as he fought to not take over the fucking. His fingers dug into her hips and would probably leave faint bruises. Bruises she would treasure.

"You feel so good inside me," she whispered in his ear. "So good. So thick. So hot."

Lucas groaned and went wild. He gripped her ass and led her in a wild ride that left her with no recourse but to hang on. Grasping his shoulders, she leaned her head back, let him lift and drag her down his cock, stroking into her over and over again. His hips thrust high with each downward plunge of hers, and the arias of her wet sex releasing him, flesh smacking flesh, and her broken cries filled the room in the most beautiful opera. Over and over, she welcomed and clasped in the most intimate of embraces, his cock marking her each time he buried it within her.

"Come for me, sweetheart," he breathed against her throat. "And take me with you." He reached between them, rubbed a thumb over her clit, circling the bundle of nerves three times before catapulting her into a sea of rapture.

When her head eventually crested the tempestuous waves, he bucked beneath her, straining, pumping, and spilling in short, powerful bursts. She clung to him. Depended on him to buoy her up, and he did. Even as the fire raged, simmered, than banked, he wrapped her in his arms.

And with her cheek pressed to his damp shoulder, she asked the question that had lurked in the back of her mind since he'd trusted her with his truth.

"Lucas?"

"Yes?" He rubbed a palm up her spine and back down in a calming caress.

"Your father's partner and best friend. The one who cheated with your mother." She paused, suspecting the answer as she asked. "It was Dad, wasn't it?"

A pause.

"Yes."

Grief, pain, and shame exploded inside her chest like emotional shrapnel. The cheating part didn't surprise her; Jason's issues with faithfulness had been a poorly kept secret around their house. But cheating his best friend out his livelihood while he was holed up in grief? Even as emotionally distant and critical as her father had become, she still couldn't match up the cold, conniving man Lucas described with the man she'd known.

A shudder ripped through her, and she curled her fingers into Lucas's waist as if trying to hold on to something she'd never really had.

A chance.

"I'm sorry," she whispered, barely able to push the apology past the thickness in her throat.

His hand paused in its soothing motion on her back.

"It's not your fault, sweetheart."

She didn't reply. Didn't point out the irony in his statement, since he'd made her pay part of the price for her father's sins. Despair weighed down on her like an anvil.

For a moment, a glimmer of hope had flickered inside her. But now, that glow had been snuffed out by the sense that she and Lucas had been doomed before they ever started.

Chapter Eighteen

How many of these events was a man required to suffer through before granted a pardon? Hell, they all started to run together after a while. Given where Lucas had grown up, he donated to foundations championing literacy, education, and technology in inner-city schools. But he would much rather have stayed home with Sydney tonight. Even watching one of those crime shows she enjoyed so much. Anything rather than attending another gala—was this one for animal shelters?—and spending time schmoozing. Or zoning out.

Like now.

He nodded and uttered the appropriate sympathetic reply when Mrs. Anita Gamble—wife of one of the wealthiest financiers along the East Coast—launched into another diatribe regarding the ill treatment of her beautiful shih tzu, Precious, at the hands of the groomer.

Jesus. Really? But he smiled, made the proper concerned responses and noises. He grinned and bore it all the while wondering when the brain bleed would begin.

In Chicago, he'd attended his fair share of social galas and parties, but as a single man and businessman, an absence or four could be excused. Not so as a married man. And definitely not for a man married under the scarlet banner of scandal.

Tuning out Mrs. Gamble's views on going "American" with groomers, he scanned the room for his wife. *There.* Surrounded by a bevy of women who flickered and faded into his peripheral vision. With her gorgeous curls tamed into a sexy sweep over a bare shoulder, she outshone every woman in the room. The curves he'd developed an obsession for were displayed to perfection in an elegant black-and-white corseted gown that hugged her breasts and small waist before falling dramatically to the floor. He, who admittedly knew shit about fashion, appreciated the flair of the dress. But it was the woman who made it unforgettable.

The warmth that blended with the sharper heat of desire both unnerved and settled him. Ever since he'd revealed his true history to her earlier that week, the unsettling emotion had taken root and had been impossible to eradicate. At some point in the study, he'd stopped viewing his wife as transitory and started thinking of her as more permanent.

And that scared the shit out of him.

He lost focus around her. Hell, he'd skipped out on work just to be with her. She made him question his every belief about women and marriage. And that kind of uncertainty — specifically at this critical time — was dangerous. Yes, Sydney was different from any woman he'd ever met. Yet he still hadn't revealed the entire extent of his plans regarding her father. Why? Did he simply not want her to look at him with hatred? Or did a part of him continue to mistrust her?

Maybe a turbulent mixture of both.

"Penny for your thoughts," a sultry voice intruded on his brooding. He blinked, realizing Mrs. Gamble had moved on and Caroline Dresden stood in her stead. "Or are yours more expensive?"

"Hello, Caroline," he greeted, ignoring the heat in the brunette's scrutiny. "How are you?"

Her red-painted lips turned down in a pout he might have once found sexy but that now annoyed him. "You can ask me that after you've become a married man?" She ran a crimson fingernail down the lapel of his tuxedo jacket. "I will be the first to admit, I didn't believe you would actually go through with the marriage. But when you settle your mind on something, you always get it, don't you, Lucas?" she murmured, glancing up at him through the thick fringe of her lashes. "I remember how it felt to be on the receiving end of that…determination."

Clearly she was into revising history. From what he re-called—and honestly, it wasn't much—she hadn't been diffi-cult to pursue or catch. Gently but firmly removing her hand from him, he drawled, "And I don't remember you being this tenacious—or hard of hearing. I'm married."

Anger brightened her gaze for a moment before she covered the quicksilver emotion with another catlike smile. It was a wonder feathers weren't poking out between her perfect teeth.

"Happily married, though?" she purred, setting off a warning tingle. One of the reasons he'd ended their short association was due to her manipulations. She didn't say or do anything without purpose. "I heard the honeymoon might be over before it even started. More so since your wife was seen with Tyler Reinhold only a week ago." She named the restaurant where Sydney had met her mother at for lunch. "A cozy lunch? Maybe reconciliation was the day's special?"

He arched an eyebrow, feigning disinterest when inside his stomach clenched, twisted. Anger and the grime-coated stain of suspicion spread inside his chest. "Spreading gossip, Caroline?" He tsked. "Business must be slow."

Her tinkled laughter grated over his nerves like a rusty blade. "Not at all. I'm never too busy to be concerned. Oh, hello, Sydney," she cooed as his wife appeared at his side, her hand resting on the inside of his elbow. "Belated congratulations on your marriage."

"Thank you," Sydney said, her tone cool.

"I was delighted you two could come tonight. Though I must admit I was surprised to see you." A perplexed frown appeared between Caroline's brows, an expert mimicry of concern. "A friend of mine told me you'd already RSVP'd to the reception the Reinholds are holding after tonight's ballet."

If he hadn't been so in tune to Sydney, he would've missed the subtle stiffening of her body. Maybe he imagined it, but that insidious suspicion hissed in his head that he hadn't. He wanted to tilt her head back so he could study her expression, her eyes. Reassure himself that his wife wasn't hiding something from him.

That she hadn't lied to him.

"That's the thing with gossip," Sydney pointed out, icicles dripping from each word. "More often than not, it's unreliable. Or untrue. Which is why I try not to indulge in such inane and childish pastimes." Surprise slackened Caroline's sharp features at the polite but dagger-sharp put-down. Her mouth curled into an ugly snarl, but before she could utter a word, Sydney turned to him and smiled the Blake smile. "George Gamble mentioned how much he would love to speak with you."

"I'm all yours and his," he murmured. Pride roared through him like a lion, fierce, loud. Leaving Caroline fuming behind them, he escorted Sydney across the room. As he entered into a surprisingly interesting and engaging conversation with Anita Gamble's husband, he maintained an arm around his wife.

For the rest of the evening, he tried to expel Caroline's catty remarks from his head. But when he and Sydney returned home a couple of hours later, the comments continued to loiter like ghosts refusing to go into the light. But even if he somehow managed to dismiss Caroline's sly innuendos, he couldn't erase the doubt they'd planted. No shovel or plow could uproot that.

"Lucas."

He eased her coat from her shoulders, his fingertips brushing her bare shoulders. "Yes?"

"Do you want to talk about what Caroline said tonight?"

His jaw clenched, and he turned and hung their coats in the hall closet before returning to her in the living room. Slipping his hands in the front pockets of his pants, he studied her. The hint of nervousness under cool composure. The flash of wariness in her eyes. And the suspicion stretched its poisonous tentacles a little further.

"Is there something to talk about, Sydney?"

She shook her head, and the gold and caramel caught the light of the single lamp.

"When I had lunch with Mom, unknown to me, she had arranged for Tyler to show up at the restaurant. She'd also accepted an invitation to his parents' reception on my behalf. I didn't find out any of this until that afternoon." She held out her hands, the palms up in supplication. "I meant to tell you. There was—is—nothing to hide. But when I came home…it slipped my mind. We started talking about her, and then you took me down to your study. And I truly forgot to mention it. I had no intention of going to the reception or seeing Tyler again."

He didn't reply. Couldn't. On the surface, her reasons seemed plausible. But in the interim—in the days that had passed since that day—why hadn't she said anything? His mind was quick to supply ugly reasons. Such as her intent to meet with her ex again. After all, he'd been the reason she couldn't bring herself to be intimate with Lucas on their wedding night. Did she still love him?

An image of his father solidified in his mind. Devastated, defeated. Because of his love for a woman who'd broken his heart and trust time after time with infidelity after infidelity.

Staring into her lovely face, he wanted to believe her. But his own experience had taught him the consequences of giving trust so freely, so cavalierly.

"Say something," she whispered.

"Let's go to bed," he murmured, holding out his hand.

After a moment's hesitation, she placed her hand in his and allowed him to lead her up the stairs to the bedroom. Where he removed her dress, slid his hands over her body, made her come apart with his fingers, mouth, and cock. And after their breathing returned to a semblance of normal, and the perspiration dried on their skin, started all over again.

Because here, he thought as he buried himself in the hungry, grasping core of her, there were no lies.

Chapter Nineteen

"Thank you, James." Sydney smiled at the ever-attentive driver as he helped her from the rear of the town car. Over the weeks, they'd developed a rapport, as Lucas had hired another chauffer for himself, leaving James to care for Sydney. She enjoyed his calming presence and quietly funny wit. "I'm going to miss you next week," she said, stepping onto the sidewalk outside the brownstone. "But have a wonderful time with your daughter and grandchildren."

He dipped his head, walking her up to the steps. "I haven't seen them since last summer, so I'm excited about going." He grinned, and it lit up his face. "And San Diego in November isn't bad, either."

She laughed, pressing a light kiss on his cheek. "Well, have fun. But don't let them convince you to move there," she warned.

Waving good-bye, she mounted the stairs and entered the house. Silence greeted her. Not that she had expected

Lucas to be home. He hadn't surprised her like that since the day she had lunch with her mother. That didn't keep her from glancing toward the living room, though.

And didn't keep the emptiness and loneliness from knotting her stomach.

God, she should have an ulcer by now.

Since the night of the party a week ago, there'd been a distance between her and Lucas that hadn't been there since their time in Seattle. One inserted by him. He'd drawn behind this reserved civility that warned her away. Even in the one place he'd never held back with her—their bedroom— he'd become detached. It hurt. It confused her. It left her doubting his attraction to her. Old insecurities had risen, and as a defense, she'd drawn away from him, too, increasing the gulf. A gulf she had no idea how to swim across.

She peeled her coat off, tired from sleepless nights as well as a long day at the youth center. Although she thanked God for her time at the center. There, she could forget about the sharp turn her relationship with Lucas had taken. She could lose herself in work, but now, in the resounding quiet, she had nothing to distract her. Sighing, she closed the closet door, and as she headed back toward the foyer, her cell phone vibrated in the pocket of her skirt. Her pulse tripped. How pathetic did it make her that she hoped to hear her husband's voice? Not quite you-hang-up-no-you-hang-up pathetic but definitely I-want-to-sleep-in-your-shirt-so-I-can-have-your-scent-surround-me pathetic.

Removing the phone, she glanced down at the screen.

Tyler.

God. She hit the reject button and pocketed the phone. Since she'd missed his family's party last weekend, he'd called several times. Encouraged by her mother, no doubt. Sydney snorted, disgusted. Shaking her head, she picked up the mail and, as was her practice, sorted through it. She removed the junk mail, left the one piece for her on the end table, and carried the rest to Lucas's study.

She stepped into the room, flipped the light switch, and inhaled his scent. Another silly ritual. But since he'd never caught her at it, one she considered harmless. She strode across the room and rounded his desk. A moment later, she dropped the mail on the usually immaculate top next to a letter-sized manila envelope. She stepped back, but then the name typed across the front snagged her attention.

Blake Corporation contract.

She frowned. What contract? Was this about her father? After a moment's hesitation and a flash of guilt, she picked up the envelope and flipped open the unsealed flap. She withdrew a thick sheaf of papers, and letting the manila envelope float back to the desk, perused the cover page.

Her heart pounded as her stomach bottomed out.

Jason Blake. Demand for resignation as CEO and chairman of the board of directors of Blake Corporation. Requested by majority shareholder Lucas Oliver.

What was this?

Nausea roiled in her belly, acidic bile racing toward the back of her throat. What did it mean? She flipped through the first few pages, and horror and the pain of betrayal yawned wide inside her like a dark, voracious chasm.

The doorbell chimed above her. She remained frozen behind the desk, staring at the stack of legal papers. Only when the second insistent buzz echoed through the house did she move toward the study door, the contract still clutched in her fist. Numb, she returned to the main level and opened the front door.

"Tyler." She stared at her ex-fiancé, not grasping why he stood on the doorstep of her home. "What are you doing here?"

"To see you." He nodded toward the door. "Is it okay if I come in? It will only be for a few minutes."

Bemused, she opened the door wider and shifted to the side, allowing him to enter.

"Thank you," he said. "I tried calling, but I guess you didn't receive my messages. Or"—a deprecating smile curved his mouth—"maybe you were avoiding them. Not that I could blame you."

Rabbit hole. At what point had she jumped feetfirst into it? She pinched and massaged her forehead as if the motion could clear away the wool wrapping that had enclosed her since finding the documents on Lucas's desk. Turning to face Tyler, she closed the door behind her.

"I'm sorry, Tyler. You have me at a loss."

"I can imagine." He dragged a hand over his close-cropped dark curls. "Look, I won't keep you long. I wanted to speak with you about this weekend."

Tipping her head back, she loosed a broken crack of laughter. The pain from her discovery still thrummed inside her like another heartbeat. Jesus, she didn't need this right now. Couldn't deal with what her mother had set in motion with her machinations. Lifting her head, she spread her hands wide.

"I'm sorry you were misled, but I had no intention of attending the party. Mom, without my knowledge, accepted the invitation on my behalf. I hate that I hurt you and your parents' relationship with mine, but I'm married—I married another man, and I would not have disrespected him by going to your party without him."

"I know," he said. "Which is why I came to apologize to you."

If he'd sprouted wings and clucked around the room crying, "The sky is falling!" she couldn't have been more surprised.

"Wh-what?" she stammered.

Another of those mocking half smiles. But the mockery seemed to be aimed at himself, not her. "Sydney, before the dating and engagement, we were friends first. It's one of the things I truly enjoyed about our relationship. You rarely find the true companionship we shared, which is why I could see myself marrying you. Even though we didn't love each other."

"Tyler," she said.

"No, I knew you didn't and had agreed to the marriage for your own reasons. Namely, pressure from your family. I get it. More than you know," he murmured, almost to himself. "Yes, I was shocked when you broke off the engagement, and I would be lying if I said I wasn't hurt and embarrassed. But in a way I was…relieved." His lashes lowered, and his low exhale shuddered from between his lips. "And envious. You were strong enough to stand up and go after what you wanted. A fulfilled life with someone you love instead of an empty one without passion or true happiness. I"—he cleared his throat—"I had that. And because of family obligations, I lost her and my shot."

She gasped, rocking back on her heels. "Are you saying…?"

"Yes. I had a woman I loved, but because she didn't have the connections, wealth, and name recognition that you and your family had, my father 'persuaded' me not to marry her. Sydney, my father's company is…suffering." He huffed out a rough chuckle. "That's an understatement. It's in serious trouble. But the Blake name would've been sufficient to obtain unsecured loans from several banks with ties to your father and Blake Corporation. My dad was counting on our marriage, and for me to go through with it. And threats of disowning me, leaving me penniless, and withdrawing his support from me worked. I caved. And lost the best thing that's ever happened to me in the process."

"Tyler," she breathed. "I'm so sorry." Especially considering her father's company was in the same straits as Mr. Reinhold's. Maybe worse—Wes Reinhold hadn't been embezzling funds for years.

He shrugged a shoulder. "I have no one to blame but myself. When you broke off our engagement, I kind of saw it as karma with no one to blame but myself. I could fall back on the excuse of allowing myself to be used, but that would be lying. I was too much of a coward to lose my lifestyle. Anyway." He heaved a sigh. "You won't have to worry about any more situations like the ambush at lunch or the reception. Old habits die hard, so I agreed to go along with it at first. But when you didn't show up, I was glad. You deserve your happiness, Sydney, and I or my parents will no longer interfere with it."

"Thank you," she whispered. Tears stung her eyes for his loss, his pain…hers. She hadn't ended their engagement for love, as he believed, but she did love now. With a strength that transformed her knees to wobbly columns of water.

She grappled for the end of the banister, leaning against it, truth slamming into her with the force and subtlety of a sledgehammer.

She loved Lucas.

And knowing the fullness of it, the ache of it, the consuming power of it, she would have ultimately resented Tyler and grown bitter. Ironic how she'd been set on marrying him to avoid ending up like her mother, and that would have been the likely outcome anyway.

"Sydney." He darted over to her, cupping her shoulder. "Are you okay?"

Mute, she nodded, while inside she raged, *hell, no!* She wasn't okay. Far from it. She was angry, scared, hurt, disillusioned…and in love.

Oh, shit.

"You don't look well," he said, concern drawing his brows down in a frown. "Here, have a seat." Lowering her to a step, he hunkered down in front of her, his hands clasping hers. "Is there anything I can get you?"

"The fuck out of my house," a dark voice rumbled from the doorway.

She jerked her head up. Met a menacing, glittering gaze.

Lucas was home.

Chapter Twenty

Rage poured through Lucas. It pounded against his senses in relentless waves, growing stronger and wilder with every second Tyler Reinhold remained crouched before his wife, holding her hands.

Sydney snatched free of her ex's grip, guilt flashing across her face.

"I'll go," Tyler said, his wary gaze never leaving Lucas. Smart man. "Sydney, are you going to be okay?"

"Yes," she murmured. She, too, studied him with those lovely hazel eyes—lovely, deceitful eyes. He clenched his fist until he swore the skin would split over his knuckles. "Please go. And thank you for coming by."

"Of course." Tyler skirted past Lucas and ducked out the door. Though every cell in his being roared he beat the shit out of the other man, Lucas didn't move, didn't take his scrutiny off the woman who'd made him promise fidelity only to betray that promise herself.

He should've known.

"Lucas." Sydney rose from the step, holding a trembling hand out toward him. Tired. She appeared tired, worn down…and hurt. He bit back a bark of laughter. What a hell of an actress he was married to. "It's not—"

"No, no, wait. Let me finish. I've heard it many times, after all." In the beginning, his mother had tried to offer up excuses. After a while, she'd stopped pretending she wasn't cheating, and the explanations stopped coming. "It's not what I think. I should believe you, not my lying eyes. Or how about, 'we weren't doing anything'?"

She dropped her arm, shaking her head. "Lucas, he came by to apologize. That's all. I would never betray you. Certainly not after…" She inhaled. "I wouldn't."

"Wouldn't return to the man you had lunch with behind my back? The man who you'd been ready to spend your life with? A man whose memory was so precious to you, you couldn't bear to have sex with me on our wedding night? Is this the man you wouldn't go back to?"

"I didn't love him. I've never loved him. I lo—" She broke off, wrapping her arms around her chest.

"You what?" he demanded. But she just shook her head again.

A part of him wanted to grab her, demand she supply him with a good reason for Tyler being in his home—their home—and make him believe her. But that foolish part of him had also convinced him to leave work, go home early, and reconcile with her. Tell her he no longer wanted the distance that had sprung up between them. While he'd been intent on reaffirming what they'd shared, she'd been with her ex-fiancé.

For years, he'd had a ringside seat to the clusterfuck that

had been his parents' marriage. And yet he'd still started to trust, to believe a woman could be loyal…faithful. Maybe he was too much like his father after all.

He strode past her toward his study and the bottles of bourbon waiting for him.

"You don't get to walk away from me yet," she stated, and the soft, stark command plummeted into the room like a meteor slamming into earth. Slowly, he pivoted around. Sydney lowered her arms, and that's when he noticed the papers clutched in her fingers. "You don't want to listen to anything I have to say because you're intent on punishing me for a sin committed years ago. I'm not your mother. I would never take something so precious between us and pervert and twist it by sleeping with another man. You've never let go of what she did, never forgiven her for it. And now I'm paying the price. That's one strike." She shifted closer to him, her chin notched high. And fury, not sorrow, darkened her gaze. It blazed up at him, hot, accusatory. "But don't you call me a liar or tell me I've betrayed you when that's all you've done from the first day we met."

She slapped the papers into his chest, and he had no choice but to catch them or they would've fluttered to the floor. Oh, damn. The contract pushing Jason Blake out. But how…? He curled his fingers into a tight fist. They'd been on his desk in his study when he'd left the house this morning.

"You lied to me," she rasped. "You promised me you would leave my father alone if I married you. And all this time you've been planning to steal his company right out from under him, with me beside you. You. Used. Me."

"I promised you I wouldn't report your father to the authorities, and I haven't. I kept my end of the bargain."

"You lied by omission, damn it. Don't split hairs with me." She paced away from him, rubbing her hands over her arms as if chilled. "Were you going to tell me?" Before he could reply, she laughed. The brittle edge of it scraped over his skin, pierced his heart. "Of course not. That would be truthful, and as you warned me, the only way to fight is dirty."

"Sydney, this has nothing to do with you," he gritted out, wondering why he bothered to explain. She was going to leave. They all did.

"Nothing to do with me? Are you serious? You're planning to ruin my father, and it has nothing to do with me? God, Lucas. Do you think this is what your father wanted for you? To turn around and inflict on someone else the same pain and betrayal he suffered?"

"You don't know what you're talking about," he snapped. "You know nothing—"

The peal of his cell phone reverberated. He snatched it from his pocket, saw Aiden's name, and sent the call to voicemail. Seconds later it rang again. Aiden.

"Damn it," he growled, punching the answer button. "What?"

"Turn on the television, Luke. CNN."

None of his friend's usual humor carried through the line. No smart-ass remark for the manner in which he'd answered the phone. His stomach dipped as if he'd just zoomed down a steep hill on a bike without brakes. Terrifying.

He stalked to the den next to the living room. Without removing the cell from his ear, he jerked up the remote and turned on the television. An eternity seemed to eke by before he found the correct channel.

"Oh, Jesus," he breathed.

"…arrived at the Boston division of the Federal Bureau of Investigation. Our information is limited at this time, but it has been confirmed that Jason Blake of Blake Corporation is being investigated for accounting fraud. This morning…"

A cry ripped through the air. He whipped around. Sydney leaned against the door, her eyes like dark ovals in her pale face.

"Sydney," he whispered.

"No," she cut him off, her voice as sharp and serrated at a knife. Anger, pain, and what might have been grief swirled in her eyes. For a moment, her mouth trembled, but it firmed, her expression hardening. "Did you do this?"

He should've expected the question, should've known she'd assume he would be behind her father's arrest. And yet…yet her obvious mistrust burned him raw. "No," he rasped. "I promised you—"

"You promised me several things, Lucas." She straightened, shifting away from the door frame. "You vowed that I wouldn't walk alone. You swore that as long as we were together, you would spend every day proving how special I was to you. Special? Today you've proven that I'm not any different from the other women you've had in your life, in your bed. I'm renting your last name, but I'm just one of many women you've never trusted. You can't accept that I might be worthy of that trust, of that faith, because then you would have to admit you've been living the past fifteen years in a prison of bitterness for nothing." She wrapped her arms around her chest, but in the next moment dropped them to her sides, curling her fingers in fists. "Our contract is null and void. It was broken the moment you set all this"—she flung a hand toward the television—"in motion. I won't live my life in your prison—I won't live the next eleven months like that. By marrying Tyler, I would've settled for a shallow, anemic existence. But with you? I'm consigning myself to a sentence of losing myself to your hatred and lust for revenge that will only end up destroying both of us. I refuse to do it, Lucas. I want more than that. I'm *worth* more than that. *We* could've been more than that," she whispered.

Shaking her head, she whirled around. Disappeared.

And he was alone.

• • •

"And God said, let there be light," Aiden declared, throwing open the door to Lucas's study. He stretched his arms wide, but when the room remained as dark as ever except for the low lamp on his desk, his friend shrugged. "I guess that only works for God, then."

"What are you doing here?" Lucas snapped as he poured himself another drink. The third—fourth, fifth?—that morning. He'd been a slow riser today.

"Coming to make merry with you, of course," Aiden drawled. "How does it feel to finally obtain everything you've slaved, plotted, planned, and schemed for? I have to tell you, for a man who has won, you don't look very, uh, celebratory."

Celebratory? He didn't feel anything. Triumph, sorrow, anger, happiness. Thanks to the barrels of bourbon he'd downed in the three days since Sydney had left him, he'd felt nothing but the burn and numbness of liquor.

But even the alcohol couldn't erase the image of the devastation and accusation on her face before she'd disappeared.

And it didn't matter that he hadn't turned her father in; the guilt still gnawed at him with razor-sharp, ravenous teeth.

"You're an asshole." Aiden slapped his palms on the desk, sloshing the liquor around in the tumbler.

"You're going to have to be a little more specific," Lucas advised, picking up his glass.

"Okay, how about for fucking up the best thing that has ever happened to you? There's one."

Lucas sighed, sipped, and tipped his head back against the office chair. "She left me."

"As well she should've," Aiden snarled. Then, falling into the visitor's chair with a sigh, he pinched the bridge of his nose. In a drunken stupor, Lucas had relayed to his friend what'd happened the day he arrived home to find Tyler with Sydney. About the fight. The accusations. "You were a grade-A bastard, accusing her of cheating with no proof. If there's a woman who is more loyal, sacrificing, and kind than Sydney, she'd need to be nominated for sainthood. She was perfect for you. If you would've let her. Luke"—Aiden leaned forward, waiting for Lucas to meet his gaze—"she loves you. A blind man could see that. And I have damn near twenty-twenty vision."

Lucas tried to, but he couldn't block out the pictures that bombarded him like BB gun pellets. The hurt in her eyes. The quiet pleading. The anger. Love? He rubbed his forehead with the heel of his hand. If she'd harbored any affection for him, he'd killed it with his all-consuming desire for revenge.

And it had consumed.

His childhood. His vision. His integrity.

His marriage.

The woman he loved.

He set the glass on the desk with a hard *thunk* and scrubbed his palms over his face, stubble from his unshaven jaw scraping over his skin.

It'd been the seeds of love—planted when she'd kissed his scar, listened to his ugly history and accepted it, gave her body so freely and without inhibition to him—that had scared the hell out of him.

Son of a bitch. How could he have been such a fool?

So obsessed with revenge, he'd lied to her, betrayed her. So terrified he'd end up like his father—weak and broken by love—he'd pushed her away, rejected her. So blind to his own guilt and grief, he'd lashed out, seeking to lay blame, and destroying her trust in the process.

And the entire time, he'd missed one important, blaring, obvious truth.

He and Sydney weren't his parents. She wasn't selfish or narcissistic, concerned with her own pleasure and desires. He wasn't his father, needy, defeated, also so self-centered that he abandoned the one person who needed him most. He couldn't imagine inflicting such suffering on someone he loved—and he couldn't imagine Sydney allowing him to sink to that depth. She made him stronger. Wiser. Better.

And he didn't want to spend another day without her.

He rose from his chair and rounded his desk, mind churning.

"'Bout damn time." Aiden grinned, shooting from his seat as well. "What are you going to do?"

"Find my wife."

"Welcome back, Luke." Aiden clapped him on the shoulder. "Can I offer you one piece of advice, though?"

"What?" Lucas strode past him, headed for the door.

"Wash first."

Chapter Twenty-One

Sydney climbed the steps to her parents' Beacon Hill home, keeping her head ducked as she wedged through the throng of reporters camped on the sidewalk and street. Nearly a week had passed since the news about her father's financial fraud broke, and the media frenzy hadn't abated in the least.

"Sydney, did you know your father was stealing from his company?"

"Sydney, over here! Over here!"

"Sydney, is it true Lucas Oliver left you once he found out about your father?"

She detested how the reporters used her first name with such familiarity. As if they were friends. As if they had a right to her answers and feelings. Especially regarding her family. And her husband. The husband she hadn't seen in five days, two hours, and some-odd minutes. She could ignore the reporters, but she couldn't dismiss the hollow pit that had leased space inside her since then.

God, please don't let me walk into another ambush.

Her parents knew about her leaving Lucas's house—as, apparently, did the media. She cringed, hating that her personal relationship and hurts were fodder for the national news stations as well as the society columns. If this request to visit Casa Blake entailed another round of Operation Tyler, it would be a short visit. Yes, Lucas had hurt her with his disbelief and accusations about Tyler, as well as his mistrust and duplicity regarding her father. And yes, she'd been staying with Yolanda, the youth center director willingly offering her guest bedroom to Sydney while she figured everything out.

But one thing she didn't have to reconsider or puzzle over: she loved Lucas. With every fiber of her being, with every bit of her soul. She loved him. And since he'd appeared in her life, she'd grown stronger, more self-confident. Sure of her worth and value. No one had ever fought for him. Not his mother. Not his father. And she would have—would've been willing and proud to be his champion—if he'd let her. If he'd trusted her. If he'd been honest.

She loved Lucas—God, she loved him. But she wouldn't consign herself to the same marriage she'd witnessed growing up. She deserved more than that. *He* deserved more.

But with her father's arrest, she hadn't had time to see or talk to Lucas in the days since she'd left. Her mother hadn't understood, hadn't yet grasped that her husband had committed a crime and faced jail time and stiff fines. He might be home now on a two-million-dollar bond, but the chances were her father would serve time. Still, he was her father, she loved him, and she would stand by him.

The front door opened as soon as she approached it. She

smiled a thank-you at Maddie and stripped off her coat. After handing it to the housekeeper, she headed down the hall toward her father's study, where he could usually be found when home. Rapping a perfunctory knock on the door, she pushed it open.

"Hi, Dad. I'm sorry I was held up—"

She skidded to a halt just inside the room, shock stealing her breath and voice.

Lucas.

He rose from the couch, and she stared at him, hungry and aching. God, she'd missed him. The silky sweep of his hair against his jaw. The lean face with its patrician angles and planes. The vivid green-blue eyes and the cherished survivor's scar. And the tall, rangy body that spooned around her at night, powerful and protective. Her fingers itched with the need to touch him, caress him. She clenched her fists, the nails digging into her palms.

"Sydney," her father greeted, also standing from the chair flanking the sofa and waving her farther inside the room. "Come sit down. We were waiting for you."

Jerking her starved gaze from Lucas, she crossed the room and kissed her father's cheek before settling on the other end of the couch.

Jason lowered to his chair, and after several silent moments, leaned forward and sighed. "Sydney, this is one of the hardest things I have to admit, especially to you, my daughter. What the news has been reporting about me is true. What hasn't been said yet is I turned myself in."

Shock reverberated through her, the vibrations loud and discordant. He'd turned himself in, not Lucas... *Oh, God.* Her accusation and his denial echoed in her head, rebounding off the sides of her skull, growing louder with each pass. Yes, he'd lied about leaving her father's company alone, but he hadn't gone to the authorities…

"The guilt had been weighing on me for two years," Jason continued, breaking into her self-recriminations. "I could no longer go on living as a fraud. It ate at me, coming home and facing you and your mother, knowing I was basically a criminal. Still, the shame isn't what ultimately made me go to the FBI." Jason glanced at Lucas, who hadn't uttered a word since she'd entered the room, before he returned his attention to her. Weariness etched lines in his face, and while only a matter of days had passed since his confession, he seemed years older. "Since I met Lucas, something about him had bothered me. Only after the wedding did it click. He resembles his father, Robert Ellison."

She risked a peek at Lucas, worried that just the mention of his father's name on Jason's lips would send him into a fury. But Lucas remained as still as a statue, his expression indecipherable.

"I'd always wondered what had happened to Robert's son," Jason murmured. "And after the wedding, Terry and I did some digging—some really hard digging. It took a while and a lot of hours from our investigator, but we discovered he'd reinvented himself as Lucas Oliver, the man my daughter decided to marry out of the blue after one date. The pieces came together quickly after that. Your conversation with Terry about the company, your sudden decision to marry. You did it for me. To protect me."

Jason's face twisted in pain, corresponding with the wrench in her chest. "Sydney, I've done things in my life that I'm not proud of. Many regrettable things," he whispered, and she wondered if he was thinking about the man he'd once called a best friend. "But it would have been unforgivable if I had allowed you to pay for my crime, my sin. So I turned myself in to the FBI so you could be free. We—this family, you—have suffered so much loss. I won't have you endure one more moment of it. And I'm sorry that you've had to do so for me, and *from* me, in the past and now." He held his hands out, palms up, and stared down at them before switching his tired, sad regard to her. "Honey, your sacrifice made me realize I had to be better, to *do* better. But it also made me acknowledge that I couldn't be all bad, because I managed to raise a fine, selfless woman like you. Sydney, you deserve a life filled with happiness. You deserve love."

Tears stung her eyes even as shock froze her to the couch cushion. He'd sacrificed for her. For her future.

"Dad, I—" She stuttered, shook her head. "Thank you," she finally said, voice hoarse.

"No, Sydney. Thank you. You, your brother. You two were and are the best of your mother and me. I shouldn't have let my grief over losing Jay make me forget what I still had in you. I wasted so much time. And now..." Clearing his throat, Jason rose, clearly thinking about the inevitable prison stint that would steal even more time away from his broken family. "Now, if you two will excuse me," Jason murmured, then with a long glance in Lucas's direction, exited the study, leaving her and Lucas alone. Stunned, she stared at the closed door for several seconds before returning to Lucas.

"Did you know?" she asked.

"Not until I arrived here today," he said, his piercing

scrutiny focused on her.

"Why are you here, Lucas?" Even to her own ears, she sounded tired, wary. Her father's confession and declaration had taken a lot out of her emotionally. After their last confrontation, part of her feared what Lucas sat here, ready to tell her. And though she loved him, he'd hurt the hell out of her with his deception. "I'm sorry I didn't believe you about not turning in my father, but you still lied to me about buying up the Blake Corp. stock and trying to take the company over—"

"I came to tell your father the truth about who I was, about our marriage, and why you left me." A pause. "He beat me to two of those."

She rocked back against the arm of the couch. Why would he reveal his secret, expose himself?

"Before I met you, revenge was my one purpose. It drove me, it defined me. And I tried to hold on to it, because without my anger, I didn't know who I was. But over the last few weeks, I've discovered who and what I am. I'm your husband. I'm free of guilt. I'm more. Because of you. And I'm in love with you."

God. Hope, beautiful but so fragile hope, fluttered inside her like a butterfly battling its way out of its cocoon. "Lucas…" she murmured.

"I own 46 percent of your father's company, which makes me the majority shareholder. But this morning, I had my lawyers draw up another contract. This one signs over every share to you. You can give them to your father or keep them. It's up to you. And no matter what you decide, I'm still going to place the full influence and money of Bay Bridge Industries behind Blake Corporation to make it solvent once again. Even if your father has to step down because of his plea bargain, the company will remain in your family. Your legacy," he murmured. "I've caused you so much pain, Sydney. And I'm sorry. I never want to see hurt and disappointment in your eyes again. I know I don't deserve your forgiveness, but I'm going to ask for it anyway. Forgive me, sweetheart. And come home to me. I love you with everything I am." He paused. "Please...love me."

Love, powerful and huge, swelled in her chest, filling her, spilling out of her. That this beautiful, strong, prideful man would humble himself before her and the man he'd considered his enemy to ask for her forgiveness and declare his love for her—*for her*.

After seeing the file he'd possessed and added to for years, she understood the enormity of his sacrifice. For half his life, he'd planned his revenge, but he'd placed her above it...loved her more.

"I love you," she confessed, voice soft, trembling. Then stronger, louder. "I love you."

With a groan, he launched himself across the length of the couch, crushing his mouth to hers. As always, she opened to him, accepting him, embracing him. The kiss was familiar and new. Their present and future.

"Say it again," he whispered against her lips. "Please. I need to hear you say it again."

"I love you." She pressed a kiss to each corner of his mouth, to his scar. "Who you were, who you are, and who you'll be. I love you."

And sealed the vow with a kiss of passion. Of trust. Of forever.

Epilogue

"How in the world did you convince him to participate?" Sydney demanded. Lucas grinned, and she groaned in return, rolling her eyes. "Oh, God. You're smiling," she drawled.

Lucas laughed, catching the irony of her words since, just a year earlier, Aiden had said almost the same thing to him at this same venue. Except this time Lucas was attending the Rhodonite Society's annual Masquerade Bachelor Auction with his wife, and his smile was one of pure joy.

"I told Aiden his taking part in the auction would be wonderful publicity for the company…and I may know the location of certain pictures from our college days that would be pretty embarrassing were they ever to see the light of day."

"That's so wrong. Effective, but wrong." She snickered. "Why wouldn't he want to join in? This is, after all, the place you and I met. Who knows? Maybe he could find the future Mrs. Kent tonight."

"Yeah, sweetheart, not a selling point."

She gasped in mock outrage, jamming a fist on her hip, the mound of her belly more pronounced. "I beg your pardon."

"For him, of course." He smoothed a hand over her stomach and the baby sleeping inside. Excitement and delight pulsed through him when he felt a small nudge against his palm. Three more months, and he would be able to hold his precious daughter in his arms. "The night I came here was the luckiest and best of my life."

A warm, beautiful smile lit her face, and he couldn't resist placing a kiss on those gorgeous, sexy lips. God, he loved her. He didn't think it was possible to adore one person so much that life without her scared the shit out of him. She'd taught him forgiveness, blessed him with a family, brought life into the darkness that had been his life.

The hostess for the evening stepped out onto the stage, signaling the start of the auction. The same MC he'd bribed to supply Sydney with the wrong bachelor number. He laughed softly and guided Sydney to their table, seating his wife before settling next to her. She glanced around, and he clasped her hand. Charlene hadn't attended the event this year. Since Jason had pleaded guilty to several federal charges related to the fraud and started his three-year sentence six months earlier, Charlene had become something of a social hermit. She'd found it hard to face the people she'd called friends, embarrassed over her husband's actions. Sydney worried about her mother but also understood she could only do so much. At least finding out she would soon be a grandmother had brought some joy to the older woman. Hopefully, this new life would help bring healing.

In the meantime, Sydney had blossomed. She'd enrolled in a master's program at Boston University to earn a degree in social work, as well as continuing to mentor and work at the youth center. Though touched by his signing over his shares in her family's company to her, she'd trusted him with the management of the assets, and he hadn't betrayed that belief in him. Just a year had passed, but the reputation and financial health of the business was improving bit by bit, so when the time came, her legacy would pass along to their legacy.

"You're thinking too hard," she whispered, her lips brushing against his jaw and setting a match to the desire that always simmered for her. He returned the caress, grazing her mouth with his and inhaling her honeysuckle scent.

"I love you," he murmured. Settling a hand over her belly and his child, he pressed a kiss to her gold and brown curls. "Both of you."

His tale had begun with blackmail and revenge and ended in joy and love.

Now that the beast had his beauty.

Acknowledgments

First and always, I give thanks to my Father, who has blessed me time and time again. Just when I start to think I've reached my limit of strength, creativity, and peace, You prove me wrong. And the best moments of my life are when You prove me wrong. Looking forward to co-authoring more books with You.

To Gary. If there is a man who is more supportive, kind, loving, and patient, he's probably wearing a halo over his head. LOL! I love you, admire you, and strive to be more like you.

To, Debra Glass. You never fail to make me feel like a glittery, princess version of Nalini Singh. Your selflessness has been a true blessing. *You* are a true blessing, and I thank you for your time, advice, that beautiful brain of yours and *Daredevil*.

To Jessica Lee. You've been my partner in this journey, and I can't think of a better wingman—or wingwoman. Or whatever. Bottom line, you rock, lady!

To Tracy Montoya. Thank you for the following: Challenging me. Pushing me to dig deeper and be a better writer. Encouraging me. Being such a wonderful editor. Always going to bat for me. Being you. And—which might be the most important of all—introducing me to *Firefly*.

To The Saints and Sinners. The best street team EVAH!! Y'all are my comic relief, my peeps, my sounding boards, and just a plain good time. I love hanging out with you guys! And I love each and every one of you!

About the Author

Naima Simone's love of romance was first stirred by Johanna Lindsey, Sandra Brown, and Linda Howard many years ago. Well, not that many. She is only eighteen…ish. Though her first attempt at a romance novel starring Ralph Tresvant from New Edition never saw the light of day, her love of romance, reading, and writing has endured. Published since 2009, she spends her days—and nights—creating stories of unique men and women who experience the first bites of desire, the dizzying heights of passion, and the tender, healing heat of love.

She is wife to Superman, or his non-Kryptonian, less bulletproof equivalent, and mother to the most awesome kids ever. They all live in perfect, sometimes domestically challenged bliss in the southern United States.

Come visit Naima at www.naimasimone.com.

Also by Naima Simone...

WITNESS TO PASSION

THE SECRETS AND SINS SERIES

SECRETS AND SINS: GABRIEL

SECRETS AND SINS: MALACHIM

SECRETS AND SINS: RAPHAEL

SECRETS AND SINS: CHAYOT